3

Praise for Rose Pressey
and her delightful

HAUNTED VINTAGE
mysteries

"Rose Pressey's books are fun!"
—*New York Times* best-selling
author Janet Evanovich

IF YOU'VE GOT IT, HAUNT IT

"A delightful protagonist, intriguing twists,
and a fashionista ghost combine
in a hauntingly fun tale.
Definitely haute couture."
—*New York Times* best-selling
author Carolyn Hart

"If you're a fan of vintage clothing and
quirky ghosts, Rose Pressey's *If You've Got It,
Haunt It* will ignite your passion for fashion
and pique your otherworldly interest.
Wind Song, the enigmatic cat, adds
another charming layer to the mystery."
—*New York Times* best-selling
author Denise Swanson

Also by Rose Pressey

THE HAUNTED VINTAGE MYSTERY SERIES

If You've Got It, Haunt It

All Dressed Up and No Place to Haunt

Haunt Couture and Ghosts Galore

Haunted Is Always in Fashion

If the Haunting Fits, Wear It

Available from Kensington Publishing Corp.

A Passion for Haunted Fashion

A HAUNTED VINTAGE MYSTERY

Rose Pressey

KENSINGTON PUBLISHING CORP.
www.kensingtonbooks.com

KENSINGTON BOOKS are published by

Kensington Publishing Corp.
119 West 40th Street
New York, NY 10018

All Kensington titles, imprints, and distributed lines are available at special quantity discounts for bulk purchases for sales promotions, premiums, fund-raising, educational, or institutional use. Special book excerpts or customized printings can also be created to fit specific needs. For details, write or phone the office of the Kensington sales manager: Kensington Publishing Corp., 119 West 40th Street, New York, NY 10018, attn: Sales Department; phone 1-800-221-2647.

KENSINGTON BOOKS and the K logo are Reg. U.S. Pat. & TM Off.

ISBN-13: 978-1-4967-1464-0
ISBN-10: 1-4967-1464-4

First printing: June 2018

10 9 8 7 6 5 4 3 2 1

Printed in the United States of America

First electronic edition: June 2018

ISBN-13: 978-1-4967-1465-7
ISBN-10: 1-4967-1465-2

To my son, the kindest, most wonderful person
I've ever known.
He motivates me every day.
He's the love of my life.

Chapter 1

Charlotte's Tips for a Fabulous Afterlife

Just because someone wants to talk with you doesn't mean you have to speak with them. Ghosts are cool. Of course people want to communicate with a ghost.

There were rumors that Sugar Creek Theater was haunted. I'd never given much thought to ghosts until they started talking to me. Most of the lights had stopped working in the basement of the building years ago. Fixing them wasn't a top priority for management. Against my better judgment, I headed toward the costume room. It was located down in the dungeon. At least that was what I called the space. The floorboards creaked with every step I took. Every time I came down here I felt as if someone watched my every move. That was why I hadn't come alone today.

I'd brought a ghost with me. Charlotte Meadows wouldn't miss out on tagging along. She was bossy and loved telling me what to do. Charlotte had been with me for a while now. Ever since I'd found her at an estate sale.

She'd been attached to her clothing. We'd been through a lot together in a short amount of time. Now she refused to move on from this dimension.

"Cookie, don't forget to put Heather in bright colors. She's always so blah." The gold bangles clanged together as Charlotte talked with her hands.

"I'm glad Heather can't hear you say that."

Charlotte eased down the hallway beside me. She watched every step she took in her black four-inch Christian Louboutin heels, as if she thought she might take a wrong step on the old floor.

"Charlotte, it's okay if you fall . . . you're already dead. What can it hurt?"

"Why do you insist on reminding me of that every day?" Charlotte asked.

"It's just a fact," I said.

"Besides, it could hurt my ego," she said.

As usual, Charlotte's chestnut-colored hair fell to her shoulders in perfect waves, as if she'd just stepped out of a salon. Her makeup was photograph ready and her white Chanel blouse and black Louis Vuitton skirt were the latest off the runway. Charlotte knew fashion, no matter if she was dead. She didn't go for vintage like me though.

We continued down the hallway. Footsteps sounded from behind me. A cold breeze drifted across my skin.

"Charlotte, stop goofing around. I've noticed your shoes. There's no reason to exaggerate your footsteps."

"That's not me," she whispered.

I froze. If the sound hadn't come from Charlotte's feet, then who was making the noise? I eased around, completely expecting to see someone else behind us. No one was there.

"This place really is haunted. I don't like ghosts." Charlotte rubbed her arms, as if fighting off the goose bumps.

That was hilarious considering Charlotte was a specter. I refrained from reminding her of that once again.

At the end of the hallway was the room reserved for all the costumes. Racks and racks of vintage clothing, handmade costumes, and various props filled the space. Immediately upon entering the area the sense that someone was watching fell over me again.

"Why did they stick you down here in this creepy space? There are no windows. One of these nights they will forget you're down here and lock you in."

"Thanks, Charlotte, as if I wasn't scared enough already."

Soon the spookiness was forgotten as I sorted through the clothing. Vintage always made me feel better and eased my troubles. Clothing from bygone days was my thing. I owned a boutique in Sugar Creek, Georgia, called It's Vintage Y'all.

When I got my hands on a 1950s hoop skirt or a 1940s party dress, all my stress oozed away. A gorgeous Dior cocktail dress and all my troubles vanished. Anything Chanel made my heart go pitty-pat. Considering my name is Cookie Chanel, I suppose that was fitting. As a child when I ate an entire package of cookies, my grandma Pearl gave me the Cookie nickname. The moniker fit so well with Chanel that it stuck.

Charlotte sat on an old trunk in the corner of the room. "What do you need for the costume? Let's get this going so we can get out of here."

"You know, Charlotte, you didn't have to come down here." I pulled out a bright fuchsia and black floral print dress and examined it.

With spaghetti straps, a full skirt, and fitted waist, the cut and fabric would be fabulous on my best friend Heather Sweet. The director had put me in charge of costumes for Sugar Creek Theater's production of *Cat on a Hot Tin Roof.* Heather had the role of Maggie.

"I can't leave you alone down here. What if a ghost gets you?" Charlotte studied her red polished fingernails.

She didn't seem all that concerned.

"I suppose I'll talk to the ghost just like I do with you," I said.

Charlotte pinned me with a frosty stare. "You just had to get in the fact that I'm dead, didn't you?"

I moved away from the rack and closer to Charlotte. "I'm just sayin' . . ."

She jumped up from the trunk. "Pick out a dress and let's get a move on. How about that one?"

"Which one?" I asked.

Charlotte gestured with a flick of her wrist. "The one that looks like the dress you're wearing."

I pulled the frock from the rack. The fabric was similar to the dress I'd worn today. The butterflies on the fabric were smaller than the ones on mine. The colors were the same hues of lilac and yellow. The V-neck bodice had a nipped waist, and the skirt was full in a tea length.

I placed it back on the stand. "Heather already has a dress with these colors."

Charlotte massaged her temples, as if ghosts could really have headaches. "Just pick something already."

"What's in that trunk?" I pointed.

"How should I know?" Charlotte said.

I reached down and examined the latch. "It's not locked."

"That's not an invitation to open it. There's probably a mouse in there."

Just in case Charlotte was right about the vermin, I eased the lid open. So far no rodents. However, I'd found some seriously fabulous vintage clothing. Who left these wonderful pieces? A 1950s fitted black cocktail dress with a low back. A 1940s sleeveless sweater in a gorgeous cream color. Everything was from the 1950s with the exception of a few pieces from the 1940s.

"Is that cashmere?" Charlotte leaned closer. Now Charlotte was interested.

"Did you see this trunk yesterday?" I asked.

Charlotte tapped her foot against the dinged-up floor. "With all this junk, how would I remember? Now let's go."

"I think that dress is beautiful." The female voice carried across the room.

I jumped, tossing the dress in the air. When I spun around I saw the young woman standing over by the door. She was probably about five years younger than me, around twenty-five. She had brown hair cut into a bob with bouncy curls that framed her round face. Her mint-colored dress looked like it had been made in the 1950s. A large bow adorned the neckline, and the fitted waist flowed into a gathered full skirt. I was almost sure the dress had been handmade by a talented seamstress. Maybe my style was having an influence on people around town. Where had she come from? It was as if she'd appeared out of nowhere.

"The trunk belongs to me," she said. "I've been stuck in this building for years."

Oh no. Another ghost?

Chapter 2

*Don't shop when you're hungry, tired,
or otherwise in a bad mood.
Your purchase might be influenced by these emotions.
Have a clear head for your purchases.*

"Who are you?" I asked.

"My name is Peggy Page."

"Why does every ghost from here to Saint Augustine and back insist on sparking up a conversation with you?" Charlotte sashayed over to the young girl.

"I would think you would have an answer for that, Charlotte," I said.

"Why are you here?" Peggy asked.

I could ask the same of her. She didn't seem intimidated by Charlotte one bit. That was impressive.

"I'm here to style costumes for the actors in the upcoming play." I gestured across the room with a wave of my arm.

Her eyes lit up. "Oh, what's the play?"

"*Cat on a Hot Tin Roof,*" I said.

"Never heard of it," she said.

Charlotte and I exchanged a look.

"If you don't mind I have to ask, how long have you been here?"

Charlotte and I stared intently, waiting for the answer.

"What year is it?" Peggy asked.

Charlotte pointed at the calendar on the wall by the sewing machine.

Peggy's eyes widened. "That long? Why haven't I seen that calendar before? That's a long time."

"How long is a long time?" I asked.

She didn't answer, but changed the subject. "I see fashion hasn't changed all that much." She eyed me up and down.

Charlotte moved over beside me again. Her gaze traveled the length of my body, as if she was seeing me for the first time. She pursed her lips together and said, "Oh, it's changed. Cookie just refuses to give up on the past."

I crossed my arms in front of my chest, partially blocking my outfit from view. "The past has a lot of great fashion to offer that we should never forget."

"Yes, and a lot of bad too. Bell bottoms, polyester, leg warmers." Charlotte shuddered as she ticked them off on her fingers.

I couldn't argue with her on that.

"Leg warmers sound nice. Legs can get cold; although I have to admit I have no idea what they are," Peggy said.

"Be thankful for that," Charlotte said.

Peggy was chewing bubble gum. That must have been some seriously old gum.

She popped a bubble. "So what's the play about?"

"Well, it's set in the 1950s."

She pulled out the gum, twisted it around her finger, and said, "Oh wow, that's my time."

"That's disgusting." Charlotte pointed to Peggy's finger.

Peggy shoved the gum back into her mouth.

"I bet you'd like the play," I said.

"So that's why you were looking through my trunk?" Peggy pointed. "You can use some of the clothes if you'd like."

"Like Cookie wouldn't have anyway," Charlotte said under her breath.

Peggy walked over to the trunk. "Open it up and I can help you with the costumes. What do you need?"

"Oh dear," Charlotte said.

Peggy didn't notice Charlotte's sarcasm.

"Well, I'm not sure exactly. I suppose dresses would be nice. I like the red one. That would be nice for Maggie to wear in the end scene."

Charlotte moved closer to Peggy. Charlotte was taller than Peggy, especially with her high heels, so she was towering over her. "So, Peggy, can you tell us why you are here?"

Peggy turned her back to us and walked across the room. Was she leaving?

Once she was back in the doorway, she turned to face us again. "I don't know why I'm here."

It looked as if she had tears in her eyes.

Charlotte and I exchanged a look.

"That's not good," I said, moving closer. "Is there anything we can do?"

Peggy slumped her shoulders. "I wish I knew."

Charlotte quirked an eyebrow. "Don't look at me."

Peggy stood a little straighter. "Hey, maybe you can help me figure out why I'm here. The last thing I remember is from 1956. I bet that's when I died."

"Oh, I don't know about that." I placed one of the dresses back into the trunk.

Peggy looked at Charlotte. "You're a ghost, right?"

Charlotte studied her fingernails. "No, I just like hanging around being see-through."

Peggy smirked and turned her attention back to me. "Did you help her find out why she's a ghost?"

"Well, yes, I did, but . . ."

Peggy had a bounce in her step as she crossed the room. "Good. You can help me."

Yes, I suppose it was now my fate in life to help the ghosts. I didn't mind really. After all, I would want someone to do the same for me.

"Okay, I'll help, but you'll have to tell me what you remember about your last day alive."

Peggy frowned. "I don't remember anything."

"Nothing?" Charlotte quirked an eyebrow again.

Peggy tossed her hands up. "No. It's as if I have amnesia."

"I've heard about that happening," I said. "Ghosts lose their memory. In fact, Charlotte couldn't remember a lot of things."

Charlotte scowled, as if I wasn't supposed to mention any imperfection she ever had.

I'd read about it in a book too. One that I'd borrowed from my best friend's occult shop. A medium had written about the ghosts that she had interacted with, and some of them couldn't remember a thing. It would be a good thing if I could help Peggy finally bring back all her memories.

"This is so nice of you. Thank you so much," Peggy said.

When she looked at me with her big brown eyes and said such sweet things, how could I refuse?

"Yes, I suppose I could help you," I said.

"As if there was ever any doubt," Charlotte said.

A scream rang out and we froze.

Chapter 3

Charlotte's Tips for a Fabulous Afterlife

=====

Avoid the bad spirits. Don't talk to them, period.
Need I say more?

"What was that?" Charlotte asked, clutching her chest. "This is a wild bunch around here. Haven't they learned how to act in public?"

"I don't know what happened, but I need to find out." I ran for the stairs with the ghosts following close behind.

After fumbling my way down the long dark hallway, I almost stumbled as I raced up the stairs. My best friend Heather Sweet was up there. What if something had happened to her? Maybe there was an accident. I was hoping it was something as simple as they'd seen a mouse or spider. Once at the top of the stairs, I burst out into the seating area.

A crowd had gathered by the front of the stage. Something had happened and it didn't look good. Worse yet, I hadn't seen Heather. As I neared the stage, I spotted the body on the floor. Much to my relief, it wasn't Heather. I couldn't make out who was on the ground. The person was male I guessed by the dark gray suit and shoes.

"Why is everyone standing around?" Peggy asked.

People were blocking the view of the man's face. I scanned the crowd and spotted Heather standing right next to the man's body. I saw the man's face. I recognized him right away. It was Morris Palmer. A knife was protruding from his chest. Blood covered Heather's hands. Was it bad that I was thinking about her getting blood on the gorgeous cherry-colored Dior dress? Yes, that was definitely bad. I scolded myself for the thought. I suppose the blood would blend right in with the color of the fabric.

I'd never seen that kind of expression on her face. She looked absolutely stunned. Soon the gathering of people turned their attention to Heather. I knew what they were thinking. It wasn't possible.

"This doesn't look good," Charlotte said as she stood beside me.

No, it didn't look good at all. I ran over to Heather. She stumbled back, looking down at her hands.

"I think she's going to faint," Charlotte said.

I grabbed Heather and guided her away from the stage.

First we had to get the blood off her hands. Next we'd get her to a chair. My mind raced with thoughts of how the blood had gotten on her hands. How had this happened to Morris?

"The police are on the way," a man from the crowd announced.

Immediately thoughts of Dylan popped into my mind. Detective Dylan Valentine and I had been seeing each other for a while now. He would be the first on the scene for a death investigation. Unfortunately, I was one of the first too.

I guided Heather to the ladies' room so she could wash her hands. Maybe the police would want to see that blood was all over her hands, but I didn't want to leave Heather in that condition. She had already been through enough. Heather's whole body shook as she stood in front of the sink. I turned on the faucet and directed her hands under the water. The crimson color faded as it mixed with the water and circled the drain before disappearing.

"This does not look good, Cookie," Charlotte said as she stood by one of the stalls.

Peggy remained silent as she stood by the door watching us. I imagine we had completely shocked her. Once Heather had dried off her hands, she stared at her reflection in the mirror. Tears ran down her cheeks. I hated to see her like this. Maybe she didn't want to talk about it, but I had to know.

"What happened?" I asked.

Heather turned to me. "When I came from

backstage I saw him on the floor. I ran over to him and tried to help him, but it was too late."

She placed her head in her hands. I reached out and embraced Heather. All I could do was tell her that everything was okay.

"So she didn't kill him? Whew, that's a relief," Charlotte said.

"Cookie, are you in there?" Dylan's voice came from the other side of the door.

"Uh-oh," Charlotte said, racing over to the door.

"Okay, don't panic," I said.

"Do they think I killed Morris?" Fear flashed in Heather's green eyes.

"Well, the blood all over your hands sure was a good clue," Charlotte said.

I glared at her.

"It doesn't look good, does it?" Peggy said.

Oh great, now she was helping Charlotte.

"We'll just go explain everything to Dylan. He'll understand. He knows you and that you'd never do anything like murder."

"She has threatened to kill me," Charlotte said.

"She was only joking, Charlotte. Besides, you're already dead. How could she kill you?"

"Cookie, are you talking to Charlotte or Heather?" Dylan asked.

"Both," I said.

"I knew Dylan would be the first one to arrive." Heather released a deep breath.

We would have to explain what had happened. Even I wasn't completely sure of all the facts. I knew Heather couldn't be responsible for this though. If someone had harmed Morris, it wasn't Heather. She was the nicest person I knew.

"Just remember, tell him the truth," I whispered.

The gleam in Heather's green eyes had disappeared and was now replaced with a blank haze. I wasn't sure she was even hearing what I said. No doubt her mind was a million miles away. I grabbed the door handle and pulled it open. Dylan attempted a smile at me, but I knew he was also trying to remain professional. Dylan wore the gray pin-striped pants I'd given him with a plain white tailored shirt. He had loosened his red neck tie. I'd given the tie to him for Valentine's Day. His dark hair had a fresh cut. I knew because I'd gone with him last night to his salon appointment.

"Are you all okay?" he asked.

Physically yes, but mentally . . . I motioned toward Heather with a tilt of my head. Police swarmed the area. They stood around Morris, peering down at his lifeless body.

"Come with me and sit down." Dylan gestured toward the chairs away from the stage.

Silence lingered between us for a bit when we

sat down. If he was waiting for Heather to talk first we would be waiting for a long time.

After a couple more seconds, Dylan said, "Can you explain exactly what happened?"

Heather still stared straight ahead.

When I saw that she wasn't talking, I said, "Well, she found Morris that way."

"Look at her. She's practically a zombie now," Charlotte said.

"Do you think she really killed him?" Peggy whispered to Charlotte.

I thought about responding, but Charlotte answered correctly.

Charlotte moved over to Heather and pretended to pat her shoulder. "There, there, Heather, it will be okay. I find Heather annoying, but she would never murder someone."

That was the most empathy Charlotte would offer. Heather frowned and looked around as if she'd felt Charlotte's presence.

Dylan touched my hand. "I'm sorry, Cookie, but we'll have to take Heather to the station to ask more questions."

Needless to say, I was upset. Why would he do that? Couldn't he just take our word for it? He knew I wouldn't lie, didn't he?

"This is ridiculous, Dylan," I said.

"Uh-oh, trouble in paradise," Charlotte said.

"It's okay, Cookie." Heather's voice was almost a whisper.

"Cookie, please, I have to do this," Dylan said.

Dylan pushed to his feet and helped Heather up from the chair. Her eyes seemed blank as she stared straight ahead. I'd never seen her like this.

"I don't think she's in any condition to go to the police station," I said, stepping in front of them.

"Cookie, she has to go." Dylan looked me straight in the eyes.

"I think he's telling you to butt out of the investigation," Charlotte said.

"You should take the hint," Peggy added.

Another smart-tongued ghost. Just what I needed.

"Cookie, I promise everything will be fine," Dylan said. "After we ask the questions she'll be able to go."

I wasn't so sure I believed him.

This was the first time I'd doubted Dylan. He was taking my best friend in for questioning for a murder. He had to understand why I would be upset. Dylan guided Heather toward the exit. I reluctantly followed behind. The ghosts happily trailed along too. It was unavoidable to pass the body again. Morris was covered with a white sheet while police talked and blocked off the area. I cast a quick peek, but I didn't want to look too long. We stepped outside and Dylan put Heather in the back of his car.

"In the back? Is that really necessary?" I asked.

"It's just procedure," Dylan said, shutting the door.

I didn't like the looks of this.

"I'll follow you there, Heather," I called out.

With the door closed and window up, it didn't look as if she even heard me.

Before Dylan said another word I hurried over and hopped in my 1948 Buick convertible. My grandfather had given me the car. It was in mint condition just as he'd left it. Leather seats and shiny chrome. Charlotte was in the passenger seat as usual. I jumped when I looked in the rearview mirror. Peggy was sitting in the backseat. I'd momentarily forgotten about her. It was no surprise with the shocking turn of events. At one time having a ghost appear would have been shocking. My best friend being suspected of murder trumped that though.

"My father had a car just like this," Peggy said as she ran her hand along the back of the seat. "The leather seats are keen."

I should have guessed Peggy would come with me.

"Thank you," I said as I pulled onto the road.

The fuzzy dice dangling from the rearview mirror swung wildly as I punched the gas, trying to catch up with Dylan's car.

"What clues would they have that your friend murdered that man?" Peggy asked.

"None that I can think of," I said.

"We found her standing over the body with blood all over her," Charlotte said.

"Yes, but she said she tried to help him." I navigated a curve.

"Do you think the police will actually believe that?" Peggy said.

I peered at her in the rearview mirror. She wasn't making this any easier. She was starting to sound like Charlotte. Peggy was right though. Just because I knew Heather wasn't capable of murder didn't mean the police would believe that. Dylan knew Heather though. Wouldn't he know the truth? Plus, if I told him Heather didn't do it he should believe me.

"I suppose they'll find fingerprints on the murder weapon," Charlotte said.

"I hope so," I said.

"Unless they're your friend's fingerprints," Peggy said.

Whose side was she on anyway?

"The killer could have worn gloves," Charlotte said.

Where did the killer go? How soon had the murder occurred before Heather found Morris? I had so many questions. I steered into the parking lot of the Sugar Creek Police Department.

I'd been to this building more times than I'd wanted recently.

"That's what we have to find out," Charlotte said.

"Everything looks so different," Peggy said as she gazed around the surroundings. "This used to be a farm."

"I actually sold this property so they could build the new jail," Charlotte said as she sat a little straighter. "I was a successful business-woman," she told Peggy.

I hurried for the door with the ghosts beside me. At least Dylan knew about my ability to talk with ghosts now. Though I hadn't had a chance to tell him about Peggy yet. Speaking of Peggy, there was still that little matter of why she was hanging around the theater. I wondered why Morris's ghost hadn't appeared. If he'd shown up he might be able to tell me who had murdered him. Though Charlotte hadn't been able to tell me who her murderer was. Ghosts had a hard time with memory of dramatic events.

Once inside the station, I rushed over to the counter.

"Hi, Cookie. Dylan will be with you soon," the officer behind the counter said.

"Cookie, dear, you do realize you are now known at the police station. This is never a good thing," Charlotte said while wiggling her index finger at me.

It wasn't as bad as Charlotte made it sound, was it?

"Thank you for reminding me," I said.

The officer watched as I sat down in a chair in the waiting area. He offered a slight grin.

"He probably thinks you are bonkers."

"Thanks a lot," I said to Charlotte as I looked down at my phone. "You are just full of compliments today."

"He can still probably see your mouth moving." Charlotte sat next to me.

"Don't talk to me so I won't have to answer back." I tapped my foot against the floor while I waited.

"Will you stop that? You're making me nervous." Charlotte rubbed her temples.

Dylan appeared from around the corner.

"Thank goodness. Now maybe you'll calm down," Charlotte said.

I jumped up and met him across the room. "How is she?"

Dylan hugged me and said, "She's fine."

Dylan looked worried. He ran his hand through his hair. "I just can't think of any reason why Heather would do this."

"That's because she didn't. You know her, Dylan. She wouldn't hurt a fly." I stared him in the eyes.

"Actually I did see her swat one at the picnic a few months ago," Charlotte said.

Dylan released a deep breath. "It's just that I'm getting pressure from my supervisor to make an arrest."

My eyes widened. "They want to arrest Heather?"

Dylan held up his hand. "We're not going to arrest her."

"Likely story. What he means is they won't arrest her yet," Charlotte said.

"We simply don't have enough evidence for that," Dylan said.

"You tell them you want all the information they have on Heather." Charlotte pointed.

She'd been listening to her ghost boyfriend. Samuel Sanders was a dearly departed private investigator. So of course now Charlotte thought she was a gumshoe. Ever since he'd popped up on the scene of another crime, Charlotte and Sam had been an item. He'd died in the Forties and Charlotte murdered only recently, so they were from different decades. Nevertheless, they made their relationship work.

"So can she go now?" I crossed my arms in front of my waist.

I wanted to get Heather out of there as soon as possible. I was worried about her condition after the way I'd seen her last.

Dylan stared for a second and said, "Yes, she can go."

"But for how long?" Charlotte tapped her foot against the floor.

I wasn't even going to find out that answer right now. We'd worry about that later. With any luck they'd find the killer soon and this would all be over.

"Are we still on for tonight?" Dylan asked.

We had plans for a movie and dinner, but now I wasn't sure I should go.

"Maybe I should be with Heather tonight," I said.

Dylan peered down at his recently polished black shoes. "Sure. Another night."

After a pause, Dylan turned to get Heather.

"I'm sure Heather will be fine," Charlotte said.

Charlotte just wanted me to keep my date with Dylan. I sat in the chair again while I waited. Though I couldn't sit still. Charlotte was glaring at me. Peggy seemed in her own little world as she popped her bubble gum. After a couple minutes, Heather emerged from the back room.

I jumped up. "Are you okay?"

She made eye contact this time. That was a good sign.

"I just want to get out of here," she said in a hushed tone.

After saying good-bye to Dylan we walked out of the police station and over to my car.

"She's lucky they let her go. If we don't find

the killer she could be in prison for the rest of her life," Charlotte said.

I was glad Heather couldn't hear Charlotte's words.

We got in the car and pulled away.

"Do you want to talk about it?" I asked.

"I suppose I have to," Heather said as she leaned her head back onto the seat. "I think I need a lawyer. Can we go see Ken?"

Ken was the attorney in town. I'd become close friends with him recently. Charlotte liked my friendship with him because she thought if things didn't work out with Dylan I could date Ken. That was Charlotte . . . always wanting me to have a date.

"Sure we can go see him." I made a left at the light.

Maybe it was a good idea to pay him a visit. I drove through the historic section of town. Old brick buildings that had been lovingly cared for over the years lined the main artery. Tall oak trees covered in Spanish moss shaded the streets. A mix of businesses made up the storefronts. Everything from an antique shop to Dixie Bryant's Glorious Grits diner. After passing the shops I arrived at Ken's office. No sooner had I pulled up to the curb and shoved the car into park, Heather climbed out.

"Wow, she really is in a hurry," Charlotte said.

Peggy sighed from the backseat. Charlotte and I exchanged a look.

"Is everything all right back there, Peggy?" I asked.

"I just wish I could remember what happened to me or why I'm still hanging around that old theater," Peggy said.

"Don't worry, Peggy, I'm sure we'll figure it out."

Charlotte was giving me that look. What was I supposed to say? No, Peggy, you're doomed to never know the truth? I had to try to make Peggy feel better.

I hurried out with the ghosts right behind me.

"By the way, I have a new ghost," I said as we rushed down the sidewalk.

Maybe this would take Heather's mind off her problems for just a bit. It would provide a distraction.

Heather stopped in her tracks. "Is it Morris?"

It hurt to see how excited she was about the thought of Morris being here. I knew she hoped he could tell her who had murdered him.

"Oddly enough, no. There was a ghost in the basement of the theater."

Heather looked around. "Who is it?"

She always tried to find the ghost even though she couldn't see them. Which was ironic since she gave readings and pretended to speak with spirits.

"She's been dead for a long time," I whispered. "A ghost from the 1950s. Her name is Peggy."

"For heaven's sake, Cookie, she knows she's dead." Charlotte waved her hands.

"Anyway, she's with me now."

Heather slumped her shoulders even more, which I hadn't thought possible. "I was hoping Morris would be here so he could tell me who killed him."

"I wish that was the case," I said.

We stepped into Ken's office. A small lobby area with leather chairs was to the right. Movement sounded from the room to the left. A couple seconds later he appeared in the doorway. He wore a brown Brooks Brothers suit. I knew because he'd recently purchased it from my shop. Brianna said he'd come in one day when I wasn't there. Under the jacket he wore a crisp white shirt, and a yellow tie with a blue polka-dot pattern across the fabric. His look was especially retro today. Normally, that wasn't his style.

"Cookie, I wasn't expecting you to stop by." His smile spread across his face.

Apparently he hadn't heard the news.

"There's been a murder," I blurted out.

His eyes widened. "Who? Where?"

"At Sugar Creek Theater. It was Morris."

"Who killed him?" Ken leaned against the door frame.

Charlotte, Peggy, and I cast a quick glimpse at Heather. Luckily, she didn't notice my actions. It was a reflex. I certainly didn't mean to imply her guilt.

"We don't know," I said.

"But they think I did it," Heather said.

Ken stepped back into his office and to the side. "Please come in my office and have a seat."

All of this was so scary, and I knew Heather was terrified. We followed Ken across the room. Shelves filled with law books lined the walls. Two windows allowed sunlight to stream into the room. Other than that the room seemed a bit sad.

"Please have a seat." He gestured toward the leather chairs in front of his desk.

"Thank you," I said as we sat.

Ken perched on the corner of the desk. "Tell me what happened."

Heather and I talked at the same time.

"You go first," Heather said with a wave of her hand.

I attempted a comforting smile. It probably looked more like a grimace. "I heard a scream. When I came upstairs from the theater's basement, I saw Heather. She had found Morris. She was covered in blood, so you can see why someone might think she had something to do with his murder."

"Yes, I can see where that would be an assumption," Ken said.

"I didn't do it." Heather's voice came out as a screech.

"What did the police say?" Ken asked.

Heather explained the whole experience of her visit to the police station, which was what I had expected happened. They asked her questions about the murder. Of course she knew nothing about it. I was almost sure Heather was being dramatic when she said they threatened to torture her.

"It was as if the detective was trying to get me to confess," Heather said.

"Dylan?" I asked. "He would never do that."

"Uh-oh, trouble in paradise," Charlotte said as she peered out the window.

"No, the other one . . . Charlie was his name." Heather waved her hand.

I'd met him before. He was Dylan's boss. I didn't particularly like him. He seemed harsh and cold. I was just happy to find out it hadn't been Dylan doing that to Heather.

"If they call, you have them speak with me. Don't talk to them without me," Ken said.

"Ken is just happy that he gets to stand up to Dylan," Charlotte said.

I didn't think that was the case. The rivalry wasn't that bad, right?

"Thank you," Heather said.

"We'd better let you get back to work," I said.

"Do you see the way he's looking at you,

Cookie? It's love." Charlotte stood beside Ken's desk.

Peggy was next to her. "He does look a bit smitten."

I ignored Charlotte and Peggy. Charlotte was always trying to be the matchmaker. I didn't need help with my dating life.

Ken walked us to the door. "If you need anything call me."

"Thanks again," I said as we headed out the door.

"I'll call you soon, Cookie." Ken waved.

I tossed my hand up. "Talk to you soon."

"Oh, he's calling you," Peggy said in a singsong voice. "That means he really must like you."

Charlotte laughed.

"We're just friends," I said as I climbed behind the wheel of the Buick.

Ken waved again as we pulled away from the curb.

"I'm just saying if things don't work out with Dylan . . ." Charlotte let her words trail off.

"I'm glad we talked to him," Heather said.

"So you feel a little better?" I asked as I made the next right.

"Yes, I guess so. I just need to go home and shower."

"Heather doesn't sound convinced of her relief," Peggy said.

"I wondered when she was going to wash the rest of that blood off," Charlotte said.

I pointed the car in the direction of Heather's place.

I pulled into her driveway and cut the engine. "Call me if you need anything."

"Thanks for everything, Cookie. What would I do without you?" Heather hugged me.

Charlotte chuckled. "Probably not be involved in a murder investigation. Cookie was the one who talked you into being in the play."

I scowled at Charlotte.

She held her hands up. "What? I just call it like I see it."

Chapter 4

Cookie's Savvy Tips for Vintage Shopping

———————

Having a budget is a good idea.
Stick to it so you can get exactly what you want.
No unintended purchases.

I had to help my best friend. There was no way I would let her go to prison for something she didn't do. That meant that I had to find the killer. At least I had help. Charlotte and Peggy were more than willing to seek out the murderer. They weren't the only ones offering aid. My grandma Pearl wanted to help. She just happened to be in the body of Wind Song the cat. Grandma Pearl was good with finding clues and communicating through the Ouija board and tarot cards.

The next morning, I was headed into town to open my shop It's Vintage Y'all. Being surrounded by vintage clothing always made me feel better. Charlotte sat in the passenger seat as usual, and Peggy was in the backseat with Grandmother Pearl. It was hard to decide what to call Grandma. Sometimes I used her cat name, which was Wind Song. It just depended on who

I felt was the more prominent spirit at the time since they were both in the cat's body. My grandmother's spirit had somehow gotten inside the cat's body during a séance. I had a feeling my grandmother did that on purpose. Either way, I was happy to have her in my life. The cat was still there, but my grandmother was mostly in charge of the communicating.

I parked my Buick in front of the shop. The bright red convertible certainly attracted a lot of attention. The chrome gleamed and the paint sparkled under the warm sunshine. It was a work of art.

I bundled Wind Song into my arms and carried her through the door. Once inside she jumped out of my arms and raced to her favorite spot in the front window. I flipped the sign to OPEN. Summer had arrived in Sugar Creek, which meant it was time for a new window display. I figured I would do a cute picnic scene in one window and a beach party theme in the other.

The outside of my building was hardy plank, which I'd painted a beautiful shade of lavender. The inside walls were the same hue. I had a shabby chic Hollywood glam theme as the décor. After making my way to the back of the shop, I flipped on the music so that it could play faintly in the background. Glenn Miller's "Moonlight Serenade" played—it was one of my favorites. There was nothing like the oldies to make people in the mood to buy vintage clothing.

I had called Heather this morning to check on her. She said she was okay, but I heard the distress in her voice. I tried to convince her to close her shop today, but she insisted that she needed to work. She'd have to have the extra money to pay for Ken. Maybe the work would keep her mind off things.

I wish there was a way I could help her more, but I wasn't exactly sitting on a stockpile of cash either.

"You know, there is something you could do," Charlotte said, motioning toward the front of the store with a tilt of her head.

Had she read my mind? I followed her direction. She pointed at the cat. I watched Wind Song as she sat in the window. Her tail swayed back and forth. She opened one eye. My grandmother always knew when something was up.

"She will only talk when she's ready. You know how finicky she is," I said.

"How ironic. You're just like her, you know," Charlotte said.

"I still don't know what you're talking about," Peggy said around a sigh.

The next song changed. Glenn Miller again, but this time it was "In the Mood."

"Hey, you think you can turn up this song?

It's the cat's meow. Cat's meow. Get it?" Peggy snorted.

Charlotte rolled her eyes.

"Sorry, Peggy, if I play it too loud people will complain."

"Well, there isn't exactly a stampede now, is there?" She blew a bubble with her bubble gum and let it pop.

Charlotte laughed. "So, back to the cat."

"Why do you keep saying you'll talk to her? Are you all nutso?" Peggy asked.

Charlotte and I exchanged a look.

"You might as well tell her," Charlotte said with a wave of her hand.

"Tell me what?" Peggy stopped smacking the gum.

"The cat talks to us through the Ouija board and tarot cards." I rushed the words.

She scrunched her brow. "Like a psychic? Your cat is psychic?"

"That's right," I said.

Peggy scoffed and twirled her index finger beside her temple. "Bonkers."

"Actually, the cat is my grandmother."

Peggy's eyes widened. "Perhaps I should have thought leaving the theater with you through more thoroughly."

"It's true," Charlotte said. "I wouldn't believe it if I hadn't seen the whole thing play out."

Peggy continued to look at us skeptically.

"You'll see for yourself," I said.

The bell above the door chimed and Heather walked through the door. We all rushed over to her.

"How are you?" I asked.

Heather plopped down on the velvet settee. "As well as can be expected, I guess."

"You're doing better than Morris," Peggy said.

Charlotte laughed.

Wind Song jumped down from the window and over to the settee. She hopped up onto Heather's lap and meowed.

"How sweet . . . Grandma Pearl is comforting you too," I said.

Heather stroked the cat's head. "We have to ask your grandmother for help."

I suppose Heather was right, but Grandma Pearl hadn't shown any interest in using the tarot cards or Ouija board today. I didn't like to push her.

"Grandma, would you like to use the board?"

Wind Song leapt down from Heather's lap and over to the counter. She jumped up and I knew that was her answer.

That was where we had our sessions most of the time. I pulled the board from under the counter. For the longest time I'd fought having a board in my shop. I was afraid of bad spirits coming through. So far, though, that hadn't happened, and it was much easier to keep a board here for when Grandma wanted to talk.

After all, it seemed as if the bad people were the living ones murdering people. Ghosts only annoyed me by singing while I tried to sleep and popping up in the bathroom while I tried to shower.

I placed the board in front of Wind Song. "Grandma Pearl, is this you talking or Wind Song?"

She thrust her delicate paw forward and placed it on the planchette. Slowly she moved it around.

"Wow, and all this time I thought you all were crazy," Peggy said. "She really is using that thing."

"I told you it was the truth," I said.

"Trust me, dear, I never lie." Charlotte gave a smug little smile.

Wind Song started spelling a word. The first letter was an *E*. She moved on to an *N*. Suspense hung in the air like a thick cloud.

"What is she spelling?" Heather asked with hope in her voice.

I *so* wanted this to be information that we could use to find the killer. Finally, Wind Song stopped moving the planchette. She had spelled out the word *enemies*.

"Who has enemies?" Heather asked.

"Morris?" I asked with a click of my tongue.

Chapter 5

Charlotte's Tips for a Fabulous Afterlife

---

*If the person you're attached to threatens you with
holy water or exorcism, don't worry.
That only works on the bad spirits.*

After the Ouija board session we had planned a trip to visit where Morris worked. We had to find out if he had any enemies. A workplace seemed like the perfect place to discover that. Maybe it was someone at work who didn't like him.

"There will always be someone who doesn't like you," Charlotte said. "We just have to find out if the person who didn't like Morris was angry or crazy enough to commit murder."

I hoped someone who worked with Morris would know something. Morris worked at the manufacturing company on the edge of town. It wasn't exactly a dangerous job or one where he'd make many enemies. At least I didn't think so, but I could definitely be wrong.

"Maybe he got a promotion over someone else," Peggy said.

"Good point, Peggy," Charlotte said.

It was a little over an hour before the end of the workday for the company. Luckily, it was time for me to close the shop for the evening. I'd drop Wind Song off at home and head over to Morris's former place of employment. I'd be heading past my house on the way there, although I figured Grandma Pearl would want to tag along. I didn't want to leave her in the car, and I knew people would look at me strangely if I brought a cat inside.

As I shut off lights in the shop one by one, Wind Song meowed loudly. Over and over again as if someone had made her angry.

Charlotte covered her ears. "Make her stop. What does she want?"

"Grandma Pearl, I don't think it's a good idea if you go with us," I said, grabbing my purse.

More loud caterwauls echoed through the building. Someone would think I was hurting her.

"For the love of designer fashion, Cookie, take her with us so she'll stop that," Charlotte said, waving her hands.

"Okay, you win, Grandma, you can go." I motioned for her to follow me.

As if people in town didn't think I was wacky enough already, now I had to carry the cat in with me to this company. There was no way Grandma Pearl would stay in the car even if I wanted her to.

Grandma Pearl sat in the front of the car between Charlotte and me. She stared straight ahead, content that I had not dropped her off at home. Soon we arrived at the building. It looked like any other nondescript workplace. Lots of windows and not enough parking spaces. After circling a couple times I found a spot someone had just vacated near the front. We sat in the Buick outside the main entrance.

"What are you waiting for?" Charlotte asked. "The place closes soon. You'd better hurry."

I stared at the building. "I know, but I get a little nervous before doing these things. What if they call security?"

"Well, suck it up, buttercup." Charlotte motioned. "So you'd get kicked out. What's the big deal?"

Grandma Pearl meowed.

"See, Pearl agrees with me," Charlotte said.

I unfastened my seat belt and got out of the car. "I just hope someone will give me information."

"There are always people who want to talk. It's human nature." Charlotte walked along beside me with her high heels clicking against the pavement.

"I'm glad you know so much about these things," I said.

"Me too." Charlotte smiled.

"I think she's being sarcastic, Charlotte." Peggy walked along on my left side.

"I know, dear, so am I." Charlotte stared straight ahead.

Grandma Pearl strolled along behind us. When I reached the front entrance I opened the door and the ghosts walked inside. Grandma Pearl went next. Wait until someone saw the cat in here. I hoped they didn't try to chase her out. Fortunately, there was no one in the lobby.

"Where do I go from here?" I whispered.

"Excuse me?" a man said from over my shoulder.

I whipped around to discover a tall man with gray hair standing behind me. He must have caught me talking to the ghosts and thought I was talking to myself. I would ignore it and change the subject. He looked down at the cat and frowned.

"Just come right out with the question," Charlotte said. "It will catch him off guard and he'll be more likely to answer truthfully."

If she said so.

"He'll think you know what you're talking about," Peggy said.

"Is that cat with you?" he asked.

"Yes, that's my cat."

He scrunched his brow together and peered down at my fluffy companion. What would he think if I told him it was my grandmother? He'd call security and have me kicked out. No way would I ever tell anyone about Grandma Pearl and Wind Song being in the same body.

"I don't think pets are allowed in here," he said.

"Tell him to—" Charlotte's advice was cut off when Peggy waved her arms in front of her.

At least Peggy was trying to keep Charlotte in check.

"Just get on with the subject and ignore his comment," Charlotte offered.

I smiled. "I have some questions about Morris Palmer. I understand that he worked here. Can you tell me if he had any conflict with anyone recently?"

"Ugh." Charlotte smacked her head.

"Well, obviously the person who murdered him had a conflict with him." The man raised an eyebrow.

"You set yourself up for that one." Charlotte smirked.

So I had gotten off to a rocky start. I would do better. I tried not to let his comment throw me off. I was a good sleuth and I intended to prove it.

"Yes, well, did anyone threaten him or had he fought with anyone lately?" I asked.

The man frowned. "Are you with the police department?"

"Tell him you are close to the police department. That's not entirely a lie. You're close to Dylan," Charlotte said.

"Very close." Peggy winked.

Against my better judgment, I said, "I'm close with the police department."

The man frowned, as if he was trying to understand what that meant. I was trying to understand too. Why did I let Charlotte get me into these situations? I shouldn't listen to her. Although occasionally she gave good advice.

"Let him know you're friendly. Do something," Charlotte urged.

I stuck out my hand. "My name's Cookie Chanel."

"You should have given a fake name," Charlotte said. "And for heaven's sake smile more. Maybe bat your eyelashes."

Too late now. Though I did try to plaster a smile on my face. There was no way I was batting my eyelashes.

He took my hand. "Connor Bradford."

"Nice to meet you, Connor," I said.

"Well, at least now he's being a bit friendly. Maybe we'll get somewhere," Charlotte said.

He looked over his shoulder and asked, "I guess you're trying to find the killer?"

"You got it." Charlotte punctuated her sentence with a point of her index finger.

"Did Morris have any enemies?" I asked.

Connor chuckled. "Yes, he made a few people mad."

"Morris must have been a real pain in the patootie," Peggy said.

"Interesting. Exactly what we wanted to hear," Charlotte said. "Ask him to tell you more."

"Can you tell me who and why?" I asked.

Connor looked back one more time. "Well, other than being a smart aleck to a lot of people who worked at this company, he also made a client mad. This guy says that Morris swindled him out of money. It was an ongoing investigation within the company, but I don't think there was any proof that Morris did anything wrong."

Charlotte scoffed. "That would definitely be enough to make someone mad."

"What was the man's name who accused him of taking his money?" I asked.

"His name is Mike Harvey," Connor said.

"Remember that name," Charlotte said to Peggy.

I'd thought Morris didn't have enemies. He'd always been so friendly to me. Turns out I was wrong. He'd made a few people mad. At least according to Connor. Was this reason enough for murder? Now I had to track down Mike Harvey.

"Do you have a description of Mike Harvey?" I asked.

Connor furrowed his brow. "I guess he's tall. Oh, he has long dark hair. Plus, a scar on his right cheek."

"Is there anything else you can remember that might help with the investigation?"

Connor shook his head. "Nothing that comes to mind."

"Thank you for the information, Connor." I shook his hand again.

"Good luck," he said, glancing down at Wind Song again.

Grandma Pearl meowed and he looked a bit shocked.

I turned on my heel and marched toward the door. The ghosts and Grandma Pearl followed. I didn't even have to turn around to know that Connor was still watching in amazement. Once out the door, I hurried back toward the car.

"See, it's a good thing you talked with him." Charlotte checked her reflection in the side view mirror.

Still not a hair out of place. She always looked perfect.

"Thanks to Grandma Pearl for the idea," I said as I turned the ignition.

The car roared to life and I shoved it into reverse. Grandma Pearl meowed as she sat beside me. It was obviously her dinnertime. Charlotte was in the seat next to me, and Peggy in the back.

"Good job back there, Cookie. It was a rough start, but you handled it well," Charlotte said.

Grandma Pearl meowed in agreement.

"You did swell," Peggy said.

Chapter 6

Cookie's Savvy Tips for Vintage Shopping

———————

Research before you go.
If you know a specific item you're looking for,
make sure to research the current asking price.
You don't want to be taken advantage of.

Another beautiful day had arrived in Sugar
Creek. This meant another day for me to help
solve the murder. I decided to pay a visit to
Sugar Creek Theater. My part-time employee
took care of the shop when I needed to step
away. Rumor had it that the show would continue, which made me feel bad since Heather
had wanted so badly to play Maggie. Now
Heather wanted no part in the play. Lydia Parks,
the understudy, would step in and play the role.
I wanted to know who had taken over for Morris.
    It would be eerie to go back and remember
the time when I found Heather standing over
his body with blood on her hands. Of course,
Morris's death was the talk of Sugar Creek, and
how Heather had murdered him. There was
always small-town gossip, but I wasn't getting any
relevant information. I figured it was best to

avoid rumor and go straight to the source. I pulled up to the theater and cut the engine. The building was surrounded by lush green trees—plenty of spaces for a killer to hide.

"I don't see why we have to come back here again. I spend enough time here." Peggy sighed heavily to demonstrate her displeasure.

I got out of the car. "I need to ask the director questions. Plus, maybe he'll know some history about this place that could help me solve your murder. You don't have to stay here just because I brought you back."

"Well, in that case I suppose it's okay. As long as we don't stay too long." Peggy marched along beside me.

Charlotte laughed. "Way to tell her, Peggy."

I entered the building. As usual the place was dark. For a few seconds I stood there, allowing my eyes to adjust to the dim space.

"Stop stalling and get in there." Charlotte gestured with a wave of her hand.

"I'm going . . . I'm going," I whispered.

The old floor moaned as I stepped across it. Did I mention there were no windows in this part of the building, making it dark and kind of spooky?

"Hello? Is anyone here?" I called out.

A rustling sound came from the back of the room. My heart sped up. Normally, I would think this might be a mouse, but with the recent murder in this building it had me rethinking my idea of coming here.

Someone's firm grip wrapped around my shoulder. Not only did I scream out, but Charlotte and Peggy did too. I spun around. Theo Young the director was behind me.

His pale blue eyes widened. "Did I frighten you, Cookie? I'm sorry."

Charlotte clutched her chest. "Since there's a murderer on the loose it's kind of easy to see how that could be the case? Don't you think?"

"I almost jumped out of my bobby socks," Peggy said.

"Sorry, I guess I'm a little on edge, Theo." I stood a little straighter to give the illusion of bravery. It probably wouldn't work.

He studied my face, which made me even more uncomfortable. "That's understandable. What can I do for you?"

I cleared my throat. "Yes, I have tickets to the play. Plus, as you know, I'm working on the costumes. I know this is a delicate question, but in light of the current situation will the play continue?"

"Of course. I won't let what happened stop us." His voice rose.

"He doesn't exactly sound broken up about what happened." Charlotte tapped her foot against the floor as she scrutinized the man.

"The play must go on," he added.

Peggy pointed. "I never liked this cat. He

walks across the floor too loud. The pounding footsteps echoed downstairs through the costume room."

"Well . . . with the lead actor gone," I said.

"James Chrisman was the stand-in for the part. He's a good actor." Theo sounded as if he'd taken offense at my statement.

"I've never met him," I said.

Theo studied my face. "He's a nice man. Though I suppose Morris and James did have a bit of a competition going with each other over the years."

"Aha!" Charlotte said.

Peggy moved closer. "What does this mean?"

"So they've known each other a while?" I asked.

"Yes, I believe they went to college together. They were roommates during freshman year." Theo didn't look at me as he spoke, as if he was recalling memories of the men.

A phone rang in the distance.

Theo motioned over his shoulder. "Well, if you'll excuse me I need to get that call. Good job with the costumes, by the way."

"Thank you," I said.

"I hope you enjoy the show," he said as he walked away.

"He gives me the creeps," Charlotte said.

To be fair, a lot of people gave Charlotte the creeps. Though I had to agree something seemed a bit off about his behavior. Perhaps it was because the murder had occurred right there in the theater. That had made me on edge even if Heather hadn't been implicated.

"I guess we should get out of here," I whispered.

As we walked toward the exit door, I spotted someone in the room to the left. The door to the dressing rooms was open. Though I'd never met James Chrisman, Heather had pointed him out to me once. James was in the room, pacing across the floor.

"What's that all about?" Charlotte asked.

"Looks like he has ants in his pants," Peggy said.

For the sake of the investigation, I needed to talk with him. I pushed my anxiety aside and walked over to the door.

I knocked against the door frame. "Excuse me."

The man spun around and glared at me. "What do you want?"

"Whoa. Who peed in his cornflakes?" Charlotte said.

I was taken aback by his behavior.

"Can't you see I'm rehearsing my lines?" he snapped.

Charlotte scoffed. "This isn't Broadway."

"I just wanted to ask you a few questions."

He marched over to the door. Was he going to attack me? James fixed his icy stare on me as he reached for the knob. Without another word he slammed the door in my face.

Charlotte gasped. "Why, I've never. That was completely uncalled for. Who does he think he is?"

"I thought Theo said James was a nice guy," Peggy said.

"Apparently not nice to me," I said.

"That's it. I'm going to teach him a lesson," Charlotte said with fury in her eyes.

Oh no.

"What are you going to do? It's not worth it, Charlotte. We need to leave."

I attempted to block her by placing my arm in front of her. Of course she moved right through me as if nothing stood in her way.

Charlotte headed for the closed door.

"I'm going with you." Peggy hurried after her.

Poof. Charlotte and Peggy went straight through the door. I had no idea what was going on in there. Plus, I had no way to stop Charlotte and Peggy. That man would be traumatized by the time Charlotte was finished with him. It served him right though. I leaned closer to the door and pressed my ear against the wood.

"I told you I don't want to talk with you right now," James said.

What? Were Charlotte and Peggy actually speaking with him? Could he see them?

"I don't care. You cheated on me," James continued.

This was weird. I had to know what was going on inside that room. A loud crash rang out.

Now panic had set in. This was turning violent quickly.

"What was that?" James asked.

Another crash and he screamed. The door burst open. I fell backward onto the floor. James barely gave me a glance as he hurried away. Charlotte and Peggy emerged from the room with satisfied smiles on their faces. James rushed to the back of the building disappearing around the corner as if it were on fire. Was it on fire? What had Charlotte done in there?

"For heaven's sake, Cookie, what are you doing on the floor?" Charlotte stared down at me.

Peggy watched with a hint of surprise on her face. They acted as if what I was doing was the strangest thing on the planet. Never mind they had walked through closed doors.

"What happened?" I asked as I got up from the floor.

"We just tossed a few things around," Charlotte said with a wave of her hand.

"Actually, it was all Charlotte. I just watched," Peggy said. "I'm not that talented."

Charlotte puffed her chest out. "Fine. I'll admit it was all me."

"Did he see you? Who was he talking to?" I asked.

"He didn't see us. He was on the phone. Whoever he was talking to was apparently having an affair. At least that was what I took from the conversation."

"I heard that much. What did you do to him? Why did he run from the room?" I asked.

A sheepish grin slid across Charlotte's face. "I just tossed a few things off the counter."

"You should have waited to throw stuff so we would know who he was talking to," I whispered.

She sashayed away from the door. "I got impatient. Plus, we couldn't hear the other end of the conversation."

"That was a lot of fun." Peggy laughed. "We should do that more often. Can you teach me how to do that?"

Charlotte winked. "Stick with me, kid; there's more where that came from."

"We need to find out who he was talking to," I said.

"I assume it was his wife," Charlotte said. "He's married, right?"

"Yes, but I have to know for sure if it was her. And if it is his wife, then who was she cheating with?"

"Maybe he was having an affair and his girlfriend was cheating on him," Peggy said.

"It would serve him right." Charlotte narrowed her eyes.

Charlotte had been cheated on, and she got angry when she knew someone was doing that.

I moved across the room toward the exit.

"Either way, I have to look into this. Someone around here has to know, right? They've probably overheard something."

"You know how they gossip in this town. Most of the time gossip is rooted in the truth," Charlotte said, crossing her arms in front of her.

I wasn't sure about that, but nevertheless, I had questions and needed answers.

"What do we do next?" Peggy asked.

"There should be no shortage of people willing to flap their tongues about what was going on in the Chrisman household," Charlotte said.

She was right about that.

"I think it's time we got out of here," I said.

"Thank goodness. I don't want to spend another minute here." Peggy rubbed her arms as if warding off a chill.

As we headed toward the door, I spotted someone watching me. When the woman noticed we'd made eye contact she quickly looked away. She was standing by the stage working on a prop.

"Where are you going, Cookie? I thought we were leaving." Peggy motioned toward the door.

"Not so fast," I said.

The woman busied herself with painting one of the props. She'd probably seen my confrontation with James. I knew she recognized me. She couldn't ignore me forever.

"Hello," I said as I approached.

She reluctantly looked over at me. "Hi."

"Well, this conversation is moving along nicely." Charlotte's words dripped with sarcasm.

I couldn't just launch right into my interrogation. I had to approach with caution. More flies with honey or something like that. I didn't want to scare her away from talking to me.

"I'm Cookie Chanel. I've been working on the costumes."

"Oh yes, how are you?" Stacy Roebuck attempted a smile.

"She doesn't sound genuine when she asked. I think she wants you to leave her alone," Charlotte said.

Maybe so, but I wasn't going to leave until I asked questions. With her behavior I suspected she knew something that she didn't want to share.

"I guess you saw what happened over there." I motioned over my shoulder.

She went back to swiping the paintbrush across the background. "It's none of my business."

I exchanged a look with Charlotte.

"What is that supposed to mean?" Peggy asked.

Since she didn't want to discuss the scene with James, I would get right into the questions about Morris. Maybe we could go back to the topic of James.

"Were you here the day they found Morris?" I asked.

"That's right," she said without looking at me.

"Seems like she is hiding something," Charlotte said. "Get it out of her, Cookie."

I moved a bit closer. "What do you think happened?"

She checked over her shoulder. "Well, we've all heard about your friend."

"She didn't do it," I said defensively.

"Get back to the conversation about James," Charlotte said. "Remember more flies with honey."

"What was the relationship like between James and Morris? Did you know either of them well?" I pressed.

She placed the paintbrush down. "I'm not friends with either of them, but I do know James's wife."

"Now we're getting somewhere. Ask about the affair," Charlotte said.

"Was there some kind of tension between James and his wife?" I tried to keep my tone casual so she'd think I was being friendly and keep talking.

"You could say that," Stacy said with a hint of laughter in her voice.

"What does that mean?" I studied her face.

She looked around to see if anyone had entered, and said, "She's been having an affair."

"Aha. Just as we suspected," Charlotte said.

"This is like a soap opera. Do they still have those?" Peggy asked.

"There are a few left. I used to watch *Guiding*

Light, but they stopped that a number of years ago," Charlotte said.

"My favorite was *Our Gal Sunday,*" Peggy said.

This was no time to discuss old radio or television soap operas.

"Who was she having an affair with?" I asked.

Stacy looked around again to see who was listening. "Morris."

"Uh-oh," Charlotte said.

"This is a strange turn of events," Peggy said.

"I like Patricia, but she is extremely jealous." She took another swipe at the prop with the brush.

I frowned. "She was jealous of her husband?"

"Maybe, but I mean she was jealous of Morris. Apparently he was a busy man, and I don't just mean at work and here at the theater." She raised an eyebrow.

"She means he was seeing more than one woman," Charlotte said.

"He was a tomcat," Peggy added.

"That dirty dog," Charlotte added.

"The low-down rotten snake." Peggy narrowed her eyes as if Morris were right there with us.

I peeked around. Whew. No ghost of Morris appeared. I never knew when one might pop up, so I was always on guard. Charlotte and Peggy could probably go on for quite a while with alternative names for Morris.

"He was seeing other women?" I asked.

Stacy added another touch of white paint to the canvas with a swift stoke of the brush. "He was also having an affair with Marie Damon. Oh boy, if you think Patricia was jealous. Marie was even worse."

"Now I want to know more," Charlotte said.

"Me too." Peggy moved closer to the stage.

"Did Patricia and Marie know about each other?" I asked.

"I'm not sure, but if they did it would probably turn violent," Stacy said.

"Turn violent? So that means one of them killed Morris?" Charlotte asked.

Stacy gestured with the brush in her hand. "Listen, I need to clean these brushes. It was nice chatting with you. Oh, and don't tell anyone what I told you, okay?"

I held my hand up as a promise. "I won't."

Stacy collected her brushes and disappeared backstage.

"I guess this means you have to talk with Patricia and Marie," Charlotte said.

"Yes, I think a conversation with the women is in order," I said as I headed for the exit door. "Of course, I have to find them first."

Stepping out into the sunshine, I had to shield my eyes until they adjusted to the light. The place was surrounded by trees, but compared to the dark inside this was amazingly bright. I wished I hadn't left my cat's-eye sunglasses in the car. As I walked toward my car it felt as if someone was watching me. Someone could be watching me and I wouldn't even know it. My eyes finally got used to the light. I peered back at the old building. On the second floor was a balcony that overlooked the parking lot. James was standing up there glaring down at me. A cold chill ran down my spine in spite of the warm temperature outside.

"If looks could kill," Charlotte said.

"That means Cookie would be a ghost too," Peggy added.

I didn't even want to think about that. I wondered if James had overheard my conversation with Stacy. Now I was worried for her safety. If he was the killer, then maybe he would hurt her. I climbed in the car and sat behind the wheel, contemplating my next move. James was still on the balcony.

"Do you think he'll hurt Stacy?" I asked.

"Not right now," Charlotte said. "Here she comes. She's safe for now."

Chapter 7

Charlotte's Tips for a Fabulous Afterlife

Don't consider haunting your enemies.
I mean, you didn't like them while living, so why
do you want to be around them for all eternity?

Each time I spotted a yard sale, if at all possible, I had to stop. I'd found some of my best vintage pieces at yard sales. I pulled the Buick along the curb in front of the brick two-story house. Items were spread across the yard, but I'd hooked my gaze on a rack of clothing like a laser.

"What do you think you're doing?" Charlotte asked. "You can't shop; you have a case to solve."

I cut the engine. "Come on, Charlotte, you know I have to work. No work means no money. No money means I don't eat. If I don't eat I will starve and die. If that happens I definitely can't solve the case. See how that works?"

"She's so sassy," Charlotte said to Peggy.

"She does have a point though," Peggy said, leaning forward from the backseat.

The ghosts followed me across the driveway

to the side of the house where I'd spotted the rack of clothing. Right away I noticed a few dresses and blouses, so I headed in that direction.

"She sniffs out clothing like a dog sniffs out a bone," Charlotte said.

Not every trip yielded a vintage find, but I was lucky enough to score one today. In the midst of modern-day frocks, I spotted a dress from the eighties. My hand wrapped around the item so tightly that no one would get it from me.

"I believe I had a dress just like that," Charlotte said.

The gorgeous blue fabric had a deep V-neck and structured shoulder pads.

"It's Diane Von Furstenberg," I whispered.

The only time I'd think about buying anything with polyester. As I sorted through a box of handkerchiefs I overheard Heather's name. Two women standing by the side door of the house were talking. I moved closer to hear the conversation, trying to act as if I was checking out the knickknacks.

"I heard they let Heather go," the blond woman said. "Morris was fond of the ladies. Perhaps he was dating her too."

Heather would not be happy to hear this. It was probably best if I didn't tell her.

"I told you people gossip," Charlotte said, shaking her head. "They look like they do their fair share of it on a regular basis."

"They should mind their own business," Peggy said.

I agreed, but that was unlikely to happen. The women seemed happy to talk about Heather. Of course it made my blood boil.

"I just don't like the thought of a murderer walking free around Sugar Creek," the brunette said.

I didn't want a murderer free, either, but they shouldn't look at Heather, because she was innocent.

"I heard Patricia is working at the diner now," the blonde added.

"Really?" the brunette said. "I suppose she's divorcing James."

"More like he's divorcing her," the woman replied.

They looked over at the same time.

"Way to go, Cookie, your staring caught their attention." Charlotte tossed her hands up.

The women frowned when they caught me watching. I offered a smile, but they didn't return the sentiment.

"I bet they know you're friends with Heather," Peggy added.

I paid the woman for my dress and hurried away from the house.

"See, it was totally worth it to stop there," I said as I got into the car.

"Because of the dress or finding out that Patricia works at the diner?" Peggy asked.

"Both," I said, cranking the ignition.

"Now we need to go to the diner," Charlotte said.

"I am a little hungry." I pulled away from the curb and headed to the diner.

Glorious Grits was close to my shop downtown, so I dropped Wind Song at my place and proceeded to the diner. The owner, Dixie Bryant, was one of my close friends. She had been like a mother to me when my parents moved away. When I stepped inside, the smell of burgers and fries hit me like a delightful calorie-laden cloud. The place was packed with the late lunch crowd. I'd be lucky if I even found a seat. Red-and-white-checkered fabric covered the tables. Red leather booths lined the walls with tables and chairs in the middle of the room.

"Do you see Patricia?" Charlotte scanned the room.

Dixie was behind the counter and waved when she spotted me. Sure, I should eat kale, but I needed comfort food. I caught movement out of the corner of my eye. A waitress was standing next to a table taking a man's order. Since I didn't recognize her I assumed she had to be Patricia.

"That must be her," I whispered.

"Sit in her section," Charlotte said.

"I'm not sure if there are sections."

I spotted an available booth behind the man and rushed over before someone else could get the table. Charlotte and Peggy beat me to it. They were already sitting at the table. I slid in beside Charlotte. Of course to everyone else it looked as if I was eating alone. Dixie came over with a glass of water.

"Good afternoon, Cookie. This is a pleasant surprise." She looked at the empty space beside and across from me. "Any ghosts with you today?"

She knew about my recent run-ins with the spirit world.

"Actually, yes, Charlotte is here." I motioned to my right.

Peggy scooted to the edge of the seat. "Tell her I'm here too."

Dixie noticed me staring across the table.

"Um, and I picked up another ghost at the theater."

"Morris?" Dixie whispered.

"Surprisingly, no. Her name is Peggy. I think she died in the fifties."

Peggy nodded at Dixie, as if Dixie could see her.

Dixie's gaze fell on that side of the booth. "Really? That's interesting. Why is she at the theater?"

"She doesn't know," I said.

"I wish I did." Peggy sighed.

"Well, nice to meet you." Dixie offered an awkward smile.

"Likewise," Peggy said.

Patricia walked by the table with plates in her hands as she headed toward another table. Her ash-blond hair reached to her shoulders in bouncy waves. Multiple bangle bracelets covered her wrists, long silver beaded earrings dangled from her earlobes, and silver rings were on almost every finger. I guessed her height around five foot seven.

"When did Patricia Chrisman start working here?" I asked.

"A couple days ago," Dixie whispered. "I was shocked she wanted to work here. I needed help, though, so I'm not complaining."

A crash rang out. Patricia had lost a plate. The cheeseburger and fries were scattered across the floor.

"Looks like customers might soon be complaining though," Charlotte said in her usual snarky tone.

Peggy laughed. "Yeah, Patricia has butter fingers while holding plates."

Charlotte lifted an eyebrow. "But not while holding a knife? She seems a bit nervous if you ask me."

"I'd better help her. Talk to you later." Dixie rushed off.

"She's not a good waitress," Charlotte said. "Why would she want to work here?"

"Maybe she's just learning the ropes." I held the water glass up to my lips so people wouldn't think I was talking to myself. "I need a chance to talk to Patricia."

"If she ever comes to take your order maybe you can," Peggy said.

Five minutes later, Patricia came over to the table. The ghosts were getting restless.

"Well, it's about time." Charlotte tapped her fingers against the table as she glowered at Patricia.

"Can I take your order?" Patricia's focus remained on the pad of paper she held in her hand.

"I'd like a cheeseburger and fries," I said, handing her the menu.

"Anything to drink?" she mumbled as she scribbled on the pad.

"Diet Coke," I said.

"Oh, that will help." Charlotte scoffed.

Peggy giggled again. "Diet Coke can't possibly taste as good as regular. How do they take out all the calories?"

Patricia walked away before I had a chance to say a word.

"What are you doing?" Charlotte asked.

"What do you mean 'what am I doing'? She took off before I could say anything."

Charlotte tapped her fingers against the table again. "Well, you'd better think of a plan for when she returns. Don't let her get away."

Charlotte was never shy about offering advice. This was one time I would follow her recommendation. Luckily, Patricia soon brought over my food. An added bonus that she didn't drop the plate.

"Do you need anything else?" she asked in a hurry.

"There was one thing . . ."

"Ketchup?" Patricia asked. "It's right there on the table."

She'd acted as if she was ready to walk away. Now she'd had to pause, which obviously didn't make her happy.

"Be gentle, Cookie. You have to tread lightly in asking the questions. You don't want to scare her away," Charlotte said.

"Yes, easy does it," Peggy said.

"I haven't seen you around here before. When did you start working for Dixie?" I asked.

"Terrible question!" Charlotte's voice almost pierced my ears.

Patricia frowned. "Just a couple days now."

She sounded more than a little irritated. Not to mention I knew Charlotte was annoyed with me. It had seemed like a good question at the time. Now I was rethinking that decision. What was I supposed to do? I couldn't come out and ask if her husband had murdered Morris. Charlotte was making me nervous. If I didn't ask the right questions she would yell at me again. Her tension oozed across the seat.

"I've seen you somewhere before," I said. "Oh, that's right, your husband is acting in the play at Sugar Creek Theater. I've been doing the costumes for the production."

"Much better." Charlotte's voice returned to a normal level.

Patricia's eyebrow shot up.

"Oh, you have her interest now," Peggy said.

"Yes, he is. Sorry, I don't remember you," Patricia said.

"I'm Cookie Chanel. I own It's Vintage Y'all." I motioned toward the street.

Her scowl deepened. "Oh yes, the used clothing."

"Uh-oh, looks as if she's not a fan of your shop," Charlotte said.

My shop was more than a place to buy "used clothing" as she called it. Now she really had made me angry.

"Waitress, we'd like to place our order," the man a few tables over called out.

"I have to go." Patricia spun around and rushed off.

I felt like grabbing her and saying, "Not so fast. You have to answer my questions first."

Yeah, that wouldn't happen. Now I felt slightly defeated.

Charlotte leaned back on the vinyl seat. "You might as well forget it, Cookie. She's not going to tell you anything. It's not like she'll admit if her husband killed Morris."

I took a bite of my burger and said, "Yes, but maybe she'll offer insight into what might have happened leading up to the murder."

"She wasn't even at the theater; how would she know?" Peggy asked.

I munched on a french fry. "I don't know, but it's worth a shot."

After I finished my burger, Dixie came back over.

"Patricia was too busy to bring the check." She placed the paper on the table in front of me.

"More like Patricia wants to avoid you," Charlotte said.

Dixie wiped her hands on her apron. That was a nervous habit she had. "Let me know if there's anything I can do for Heather. I know she's not guilty of murder. She wouldn't hurt a fly."

"Maybe not a fly but she hurts my ears when she sings," Charlotte said. "Have you heard her version of 'Jailhouse Rock'? She keeps singing that all the time now."

"Please tell her I'm thinking of her." Dixie patted my hand.

"I will. Thank you, Dixie." I picked up the check.

As I stood from the table I noticed Patricia by the back door. The restrooms were back there too. Patricia was on her cell. Before paying for the meal, I decided to head toward the ladies' room.

"What are you up to, Cookie?" Peggy asked. The ghosts hurried along behind me.

"Whatever you're doing just don't get in trouble," Charlotte said.

Chapter 8

Cookie's Savvy Tips for Vintage Shopping

---

*Sometimes it's okay to make an impulse buy.
But ask yourself if you really love
and will enjoy the item. If so, go for it.*

"I know what you're doing," Charlotte said. "You're trying to eavesdrop on her conversation."

"Of course I am," I said.

I casually strolled toward the restrooms. How this plan would work I wasn't exactly sure just yet. I would have to wing it and hope for the best. However, I couldn't stop looking at Patricia, and I was worried that she would notice me and catch on that I was up to something.

"Don't be too obvious, Cookie," Charlotte warned.

For the rest of my trip down the hallway I kept my stare off Patricia. That was much better. Maybe I was being obvious before, but I thought I was playing it off well now that I had moved toward the ladies' room door. Patricia hadn't noticed me yet. I opened the door and walked inside as if everything was normal. Once in the tiny space, I moved to the side and eased the door open again. If Patricia glanced over she would see me peeking out the door. It was the only way I could listen to her though.

"You just look creepy now," Charlotte said.

"Yes, a real nut job," Peggy added.

Creepy, nuts, or whatever, I had a job to do.

"I'm just worried that someone will find out," Patricia said.

"Find out what?" Charlotte asked.

"This doesn't sound good," Peggy whispered from over my shoulder.

Patricia continued, "Yes, I think a few people saw me talking to Morris that day. It was right before she found him. We were arguing too. That won't look good."

"Patricia moves up to the top of the suspect list, in my opinion," Charlotte said.

"Who is she talking to?" Peggy asked.

"If the police find out it will be all over for me." Patricia's hand shook as she held the phone up to her ear.

Was Patricia confessing to the crime? When she said "all over" did she mean because she'd go to prison? I hadn't expected to hear this. Now I was glad that I'd sneaked back here. This put Patricia at the scene of the crime. As Charlotte said, Patricia was now moved up to the top of the suspect list.

Unfortunately, Patricia ended her call and turned around to look directly at the ladies' room door. There was no time to move away, so of course our eyes met. I was frozen on the spot. Quickly I scanned through ideas in my mind. Nothing came to me. I didn't know what to do. Panic surged through my body.

"Oh, you're in trouble now, Cookie," Charlotte said.

"Close the door," Peggy screamed.

I shut the door and waited. I just knew that Patricia would come in and confront me. My heart sped up and my stomach flip-flopped as I leaned against the wall and waited for the confrontation. A minute passed and she hadn't entered. Another minute passed. What would I do?

"You can't stand here forever," Charlotte said.

"What if she's waiting outside the door?" I asked. "What if she comes in here?"

"If she wanted to talk to you she probably would have come in here by now," Charlotte said.

I released a deep breath. "Yes, I suppose she would have, and I am getting tired of standing here. I'll just have to deal with it."

I inched the door open. There was no sign of Patricia. Now I had to go out into the diner where surely she would be waiting for me. With my shoulders pushed back and head held high I stepped out into the hallway and made my way down to the dining area. I would act as if nothing had happened. Everyone continued eating as usual. So far, Patricia was nowhere in sight. That was slightly more disturbing than actually running into her right away. I paid my bill just as footsteps sounded from behind me.

"It's her," Charlotte screamed.

I ran toward the diner's exit without looking back. Once out on the sidewalk and a good distance away, I looked over my shoulder. I tried to steady my breathing.

"Well, I'm glad to see you handled that well." Charlotte rolled her eyes.

"Charlotte, you scared me. I thought she had an ax or something the way you screamed."

"In hindsight I may have overreacted a smidgen." Charlotte pinched her thumb and index finger together.

"Just a tad," I said, still trying to catch my breath. "Let's get Wind Song."

When I spun around, I smacked right into Dylan's chest. He stared at me. I couldn't quite make out his expression. Was that a smirk or a grin?

"Whoa, I didn't see him slip up," Charlotte said.

"Talking to ghosts again?" he asked.

I suppose I did appear crazy standing on the sidewalk talking to myself. It was hard not to talk to the ghosts though. I wished everyone saw them.

"You should watch what you say to us when you're in public," Peggy said.

I cast a smirk her way.

"Yes, the ghosts have been following me." Heat flooded my cheeks.

Even though Dylan knew I talked to ghosts it was still embarrassing.

"Ghosts? So it's not just Charlotte?" Dylan frowned.

"Hi, doll." Charlotte winked at him.

I gestured to my right. "I picked up another ghost at the theater. And no, it's not Morris. I wish it was."

"Hey, thanks a lot," Peggy said.

"Her name is Peggy. We're trying to figure out what happened to her and why she was hanging around the theater."

Dylan looked around. It was pointless. He'd never see the ghosts like I did.

"Where are you headed?" I asked.

"I thought I'd stop by the diner." He gestured.

"Tell him about what you heard," Charlotte said.

"I just came from there. Did you know that Patricia Chrisman works there?"

"I didn't know," he said.

"I overheard her talking." I searched his eyes for a reaction.

His mouth tilted up on one side. "You overheard, huh?"

"Okay, I was listening on purpose. But aren't you glad I did?" I smiled.

"I'm not happy about you possibly getting into trouble or jeopardizing a case."

"Why does he have to spoil all the fun?" Charlotte asked. "I like Dylan, but if he doesn't stop that I might have to change my mind."

"Do you want to find out what I overheard?" I asked.

"Yes, of course," he said.

"Now that's more like it," Charlotte said.

"Patricia was talking to someone on her phone. She was nervous because she'd had a fight with Morris right before the murder and someone saw her. She said if the police find out it will be all over for her."

Dylan peered around to see if anyone was listening. "You didn't hear this from me . . ."

"He always says that," Charlotte said. "Yet he tells you stuff he shouldn't."

I certainly wasn't going to stop him.

"Oh, this sounds like it'll be good," Peggy said.

"We know about the women Morris was having affairs with. And no, they don't have alibis."

"What are you going to do about it? Have you questioned them?" I asked. "This puts Patricia at the top of the suspect list, right?"

Dylan's mouth lifted on one side in a little grin. "We're taking care of it."

Charlotte placed her hands on her hips. "That wasn't exactly a yes or no answer. He needs to get a confession."

"Did they talk with the person who saw Patricia and Morris fighting?" Peggy asked.

"Would you like dessert?" Dylan asked.

"Only if you will tell her more about the case," Charlotte said. "And don't eat too much dessert, Cookie. A moment on the lips . . ."

Yeah, she'd told me before.

"I really need to get Wind Song," I said.

"That's the way to show him, Cookie. Let him know you're not happy." Charlotte pumped her fist.

Charlotte was being dramatic . . . again. I really did need to get Wind Song.

"I'll see you later?" Dylan asked.

Charlotte studied her fingernails. "Maybe."

"Sure. I'll talk to you at dinner," I said.

Dylan leaned down and kissed me. He watched as I walked down the sidewalk and crossed the street toward the shop. I glanced back once again and he stepped into the diner. I looked over at Heather's shop. The CLOSED sign was on the window. I was really worried about her. She didn't want to talk to me or anyone for that matter. Wind Song was waiting by the door when I arrived. There was a note on the floor by the door. Someone had shoved it under. I reached down and picked up the paper. After unfolding the plain white sheet, I read the message.

Mind your own business or else.

Chapter 9

Charlotte's Tips for a Fabulous Afterlife

Scaring people can be fun, but don't take it too far.
Just because you're dead
doesn't mean you should be rude.

It was the only thing written on the page. The words were enough though. It sent a shiver down my spine.

"What does it say?" Charlotte asked.

I showed her the paper.

Her eyes widened. "Who left it?"

"Grandma Pearl, did you see who left this note? Can you tell me with the board?" I waved the paper in front of the cat's face.

She meowed loudly. I took that as a yes. At least I hoped it was a yes. I was glad Grandma Pearl was doing the communicating and not Wind Song. I pulled out the Ouija board and Grandma Pearl jumped onto the counter. She sat in front of the board and placed her delicate paw on the planchette. With a gentle push she moved the thing across the board.

"Who left the note, Grandma?" I asked.

She went to the letter *D* and the *O*. She

spelled out the word *don't*. The next word started with *K*. She added an *N* and an *O*.

"*Don't know?*" Charlotte's voice had reached an entirely too high level. "What do you mean you don't know? I thought she knew."

"Apparently not," I said around a sigh.

Grandma Pearl wasn't finished with the board though. She continued with the planchette.

"Okay, now maybe she'll give us a worthwhile answer," Charlotte said.

The letters came faster this time. A *P*, an *R*, and an *E*.

"If this cat asks for premium cat food one more time." Charlotte pointed her finger at Grandma Pearl.

Was it still Grandma Pearl giving the message?

"What's going on?" Peggy asked.

"Sometimes Wind Song comes through too. It's not just Grandma Pearl. She can't help what Wind Song wants," I said.

Charlotte and I looked at each other in shock when Grandma Pearl had finished the message.

"*Premeditated murder?*" That sent a shiver down my spine.

Whoever had killed Morris had planned the murder. So it wasn't because of a heat-of-the-moment fight?

"How do you know this, Grandma?" I asked.

"That's what I'd like to know," Peggy said.

Grandma Pearl moved the planchette with her paw again. This time she spelled the words *woman's intuition.*

Charlotte groaned. "You mean she has nothing to base the statement on? No facts?"

"Grandma Pearl always had a bit of psychic ability. Obviously, right? So if that's what she says, I believe it." I rubbed Wind Song's head.

She jumped down from the counter and went to her favorite spot at the front window. Unfortunately, the sun had set and darkness had settled over Sugar Creek.

Charlotte plopped down on the velvet settee across the way. "This is frustrating. We have to get Heather off the hook."

"I thought Heather annoyed you," I said, placing the board back under the counter.

"That's neither here nor there," Charlotte said with a wave of her hand.

I suspected Charlotte liked Heather more than she let on—her bickering was all an act. The lights flickered and the room went completely dark.

"What happened?" Peggy asked with a bit of panic in her voice.

No reason to be alarmed. I would remain calm. Outside the streetlights were still on, although from a distance. The street in front of the shop was always dark. I tried to get a light added, but so far I'd had no luck.

"There must be something wrong with my electric," I said.

"Did you pay the bill?" Charlotte asked.

"Of course I paid the bill." I pulled out my phone and used it as a flashlight. "I'll just go check out the breaker."

I'd made it halfway across the room when the front door rattled. Charlotte and Peggy screamed. I suppose I screamed a little too. I turned off my phone so the person wouldn't know where I was in the room. My heart thumped wildly in my chest, and I was finding it hard to breathe.

"Do you think they saw you?" Charlotte whispered.

She forgot that the person couldn't hear her. Even if they'd been inside the shop. After finding the note and now standing in the dark with someone trying to get in, adrenaline surged through my body.

"I'm scared," Peggy said.

"You should call Dylan," Charlotte said.

She was right, I should, but what if this was nothing? I didn't want him to think I was paranoid. He had enough to deal with right now.

"Maybe it's Heather," I said.

Since there was no streetlight near my shop, I couldn't make out who was in front of the door. There was definitely someone there though.

"Maybe they'll go away soon," Peggy said.

"Or maybe it's the killer," Charlotte said in an ominous tone.

"Thanks for reminding me, Charlotte." I inched a bit closer to the door.

Someone was definitely at the door. I could make out their outline. Unfortunately, I couldn't make out any features. What did they want? Obviously they saw the shop was closed. The person walked away. I froze for a second, shocked by the movement.

"Hurry, Cookie, go see who it was." Charlotte gestured.

I wasn't sure that was a wise decision, but I rushed over to the door anyway. Cupping my hands around my eyes I peered out the glass, looking to the left and the right. The town actually was still as most everyone had gone home for the evening. Only a few cars moved up and down the street in the distance. How had the person gotten away so quickly? Where had they gone?

When the man appeared in front of the door we all screamed. I clutched my chest and tried to steady my racing heart. Ken Harrison looked just as confused with his eyes wide.

"What is wrong with him? If I weren't already dead he would have killed me," Charlotte said, clutching her chest.

I opened the door and said, "Ken, what are you doing here?"

"Did I frighten you?" he asked.

"Just a little." Charlotte pinched her index finger and thumb together.

"Please come in." I stepped out of the way so he could enter. "I'm afraid I don't have lights right now."

Wind Song strolled over and rubbed against his legs. He reached down and stroked her back. She instantly started purring. Grandma Pearl always had loved attention.

"I saw your car parked out front and came by to check on you. Is everything okay? You're not usually in the shop this late. Plus, I noticed the lights were off."

"Well, at least he is thoughtful even if he scared you half to death," Charlotte said.

Ken still had no idea about the ghosts in my life. Would I ever tell him? Dylan seemed to accept it, and Dixie knew, but I wasn't sure I should share with anyone else. I didn't want the whole town to know. Though I trusted Ken to keep a secret.

"I stopped by to pick up Wind Song after a late lunch and got a little sidetracked."

"I know you're wondering if you should tell him about the note, and let me tell you, yes, you should." Charlotte tapped her Prada shoe–covered foot against the floor.

"I agree with Charlotte," Peggy said.

"Once I get the lights back on I have something to show you." I motioned for Ken to follow me.

"I'll go check out the breaker box." Ken headed toward the back of the shop.

I walked along beside him. "It's right back here."

Once in the back room Ken opened the panel and flicked the switch. Light flooded the room. Ken flashed his dazzling smile.

"Thank goodness," Charlotte said.

I had no idea what had caused the lights to go out. It was probably just a fluke, but nevertheless I couldn't help but wonder what would have happened if Ken hadn't shown up when he did.

"What did you want to show me?" Ken asked.

I'd left the note on the counter. "It's up here. Follow me."

I picked up the paper and handed it to him. "I found this slipped under the door. I think maybe it's from the killer."

Ken had a stunned expression as he read the note. "Have you showed this to anyone else?"

"He means Dylan," Charlotte leaned close and whispered.

"Not yet. I wasn't sure what to do," I said.

"I think this needs to be reported to the police. I know you like handling things on your own, but sometimes it's necessary to ask for help. This could definitely be a clue that leads to the killer. Plus, it could be dangerous if you don't tell the police."

"Maybe they can get fingerprints," Charlotte said.

"Good idea." Peggy walked a circle around Ken. Apparently she was full of nervous energy.

Was it that obvious that I wanted to do things without help? Even Ken had picked up on it now. A character flaw perhaps, but I couldn't help it.

I took the note back from him. "I'll make sure to give them the note."

Charlotte raised an eyebrow. "I'm not sure if I believe her."

"She did look as if she was fibbing," Peggy said, and looked me up and down.

"By the way, I've tried calling Heather, but she doesn't answer. Have you talked with her lately?" Ken asked.

"It's been a few hours. I can try to call her now." I pulled out my phone.

He held up his hand. "It's not necessary this late. Can you ask her to call me in the morning?"

"Is it serious?" I asked.

Was he withholding information about the murder from me?

Ken smiled. "Not serious. I just wanted to ask a few questions."

"Sure, I'll ask her to call you."

Ken stared. "Well, I guess I should be going

now. Can I walk you to your car? I don't think it's safe leaving you here alone."

It was only a few steps away, but I suppose I didn't want to hang around here alone any longer. Plus I had received a threatening note. The wise decision would be for Ken to walk with me.

"That's sweet of him," Charlotte said.

"What a gentleman," Peggy said.

The ghosts swooned over Ken's behavior. That was him. Ken was one of the kindest people I'd ever met.

"Sure, let me get my bag," I said.

I would worry about the note in the morning. Things would be less scary in the light of day. There was nothing Dylan could do about it tonight. That was when I remembered Dylan was coming over for dinner later. I'd almost forgotten. After grabbing my things, Wind Song followed me out the door.

"I've never seen a cat follow commands like that," Ken said.

Little did he know that she didn't follow commands. Grandma Pearl would always do exactly what she wanted. Ken walked with me over to the car. Dark clouds had rolled in, covering the stars. Thunder rumbled in the distance. A strange feeling lingered in the air. I suppose I was just still bothered by the lights going off and receiving the note.

Ken opened my car door. "Do you have dinner plans?"

"He breaks my heart. Why does he look so sad like a lost puppy?" Charlotte asked.

She didn't need to tell me. Looking in Ken's eyes made me ask the same question.

"Actually I do. Maybe lunch soon?"

"Sure, sure. Lunch would be good." Ken attempted a smile.

"So sad . . ." Peggy said.

After I got in the car Ken closed the door. I cranked the engine and waved as I drove off. I still had that strange feeling though. How would Ken walk to his car. Was it safe for him? Maybe I should turn around and check on him. I couldn't shake the feeling, so I knew I had to do something about it. I made the next right. I wouldn't be able to sleep unless I knew that Ken was okay.

"Where are you going?" Charlotte asked.

"I think I need to make sure Ken gets to his car safely," I said.

"Did you see something?" Charlotte asked. Thank goodness Ken reached his car and I could go home.

Since Dylan was coming over for dinner I knew I had to serve something other than peanut butter and jelly sandwiches. Although Dylan liked PB&J sandwiches. I'd decided to make blackened catfish, fried green tomatoes, and homemade buttermilk biscuits—traditional Southern cooking. After the last few days, we needed a treat. I'd just taken the biscuits out of the oven when the doorbell rang.

"I hope he likes hockey pucks," Charlotte said.

"Oh yeah, you're not exactly a gourmet chef," I said, placing the pan of biscuits on the counter.

Peggy leaned close as if she would get a whiff of the freshly baked biscuits.

"She's so snarky," Charlotte whispered to Peggy.

As I walked through the living room toward the front door, I spotted Wind Song sitting in the hallway. She was hissing and staring at the door. She'd never had that reaction toward Dylan in the past. Grandma Pearl and Wind Song both liked Dylan. I hesitated on whether I should open the door. Finally, I eased the door open just a bit. No one was there. I knew someone had rung the bell. Anxiety raced through me. Thoughts of the note flooded back. I glanced around, but saw no one. Charlotte and Peggy were behind me.

"Should I go out onto the porch and look around?" I whispered.

"Normally I would say yes, but now I'm sensing a bad vibe," Charlotte said, peeking outside.

"Hey, what are you doing out here? Waiting

for me?" Dylan appeared from around the side of the house.

Of course he had startled me. I jumped and a scream escaped my lips.

"Are you all right?" Dylan asked.

I nodded but still hadn't caught my breath enough to speak.

He noticed my expression. "What happened?"

"Did you just get here? I didn't notice your car," I said, trying to bring down my heart rate.

"I parked on the side." Dylan walked up the steps.

"So you didn't ring the doorbell?" I asked.

"Did someone ring the bell?" He studied my face.

He was trying to see if I was being truthful since he knew I wouldn't want to worry him. Hiding my emotions was difficult. I'd never had a good poker face.

"Tell him." Peggy motioned.

"You need to tell him about the note too," Charlotte said.

"Yes, I heard the bell. Maybe it's faulty." I attempted a smile.

"I'll have a look around. Wait inside for me."

Normally Dylan didn't wear his gun to dinner, but tonight was different. Why had he chosen to wear it? He pulled it from the holster and headed out into the dark night. I lost sight of him as he went around the side of the house with his gun drawn. Dylan had asked me to wait inside. Or maybe it was more like an instruction to wait inside. I rarely did what anyone told me, and tonight was no different.

"This is getting serious," Peggy said.

"It's always serious around Sugar Creek lately," Charlotte said.

I fidgeted as I stood by the door and waited for Dylan to return.

"Where is he? What's taking so long?" Charlotte asked. "I'm going to find him."

"I'll go with you," Peggy said.

I liked having Charlotte and Peggy there to talk with me so it was less scary, but I also wanted to know that Dylan was all right. Clouds filled the dark sky. It sent a shiver down my spine to think someone could be out there watching me right now. After a few more seconds he returned.

"I didn't see anyone or anything suspicious. Are you sure you heard the bell?"

I should be relieved, but that still didn't explain the doorbell. I knew I hadn't imagined it.

"I'm positive."

Dylan stepped over to the bell and pushed the button. The bell chimed just as it had a short time earlier.

"Could be a short in the wiring."

I studied his face. "I guess you're right. I'll have someone look at it."

"I can take a look at it for you," he said.

"Not now. I don't want dinner to get cold."

He smiled. "Let's go inside then."

Dylan looked back one more time. Was there something he wasn't telling me? I suppose I needed to tell him about the note now. This wasn't turning out to be the romantic dinner I had planned.

Chapter 10

Cookie's Savvy Tips for Vintage Shopping

---

*Just because something is a bargain price doesn't
mean you should buy it. Sometimes they're marked
down for a reason. Maybe missing buttons,
a broken zipper, or stained. If you're willing to repair
or don't mind the flaws, then it might be worth it.*

Another beautiful sunny day and I'd decided
to head to the theater on my lunch break. The
top was down on the Buick as we barreled down
the road toward our destination. Elvis Presley
played on the radio. Peggy's favorite, and mine
too. My outfit of choice today was an Emilio
Pucci orange and white cotton pencil skirt.
Normally orange wasn't a color I reached for
often, but sometimes the pop of color was fun.
Especially in the summertime. It reminded me
of a Popsicle. The skirt had bits of gray in the
abstract pattern as well. My button-down white
short-sleeve shirt had a fitted waist and small
rounded collar. Tiny white buttons ran down
the front. My Manolo Blahnik white heels and
white Gucci top-handle handbag completed
the look.

I'd recently hired a part-time employee, so she was looking after the shop while I was gone. It was hard to let someone watch over the place, but I couldn't be there all the time. Having help would free up time for me to find new inventory. Not to mention be able to keep Heather out of prison by finding the killer.

Charlotte sat in the passenger seat up front and Peggy was in the back. They were in an especially energetic mood this afternoon. As usual Charlotte donned her luxury fashion. With a Saint Laurent sea-green silk blouse with puffed sleeves gathered at the wrists. Her black Gucci wrap skirt hit just above the knees. Her stilettos were Gucci too. Peggy wore an adorable pink and black full poodle skirt and white cotton blouse with tiny pearl buttons down the front that was quite similar to mine. She wore her hair pulled back in a ponytail.

"I have a good feeling about this trip," Charlotte said.

"Me too. I think we'll find good clues." Peggy blew out a giant pink bubble and popped it, leaving the remnants on her face.

Who knew there was ghostly bubble gum?

"I sure hope so," I said.

Only a few cars dotted the theater's parking lot. I had hoped there would be more people so that I could easily blend in with the crowd. Though they wouldn't be surprised I was there since I was working on costumes, I just figured it would be easier to eavesdrop if they didn't know I was around. Would James Chrisman be here today? He'd seemed extremely irritated the last time he'd seen me.

Instead of parking out front, I parked the car in the back lot. It was for spillover cars during performances, although sadly there was never need to use it. The plays were mostly sold out, though, so that was good. I shoved the car into park and climbed out from behind the wheel. There was a back entrance that led into the kitchen. I hoped that someone had left that door open and I'd be able to slip in that way. Charlotte needed to get better at unlocking doors. She was having problems with using her ghostly thumbs. The theater sat atop a small hill, and the parking lot was below and in an area surrounded by oak, pine, and maple trees. Dense vegetation gave ample places for a killer to hide. Of course this added to my unease, as if I wasn't already stressed enough.

"Stay strong, Cookie. I know you're tense. I sense it," Charlotte said as she got out of the car.

Charlotte's intuition had increased over the past few months.

"I'll try, but it's hard," I said, locking the car door behind me.

I hurried across the lot toward the back door. For the entire trip across the lot I told myself that I was just being paranoid. There was no one lurking behind the trees watching me. After receiving the note and someone mysteriously ringing the doorbell last night, I couldn't hold back the feelings. I guess having the ghosts beside me helped somewhat. It made it feel as if I wasn't completely alone. To everyone else I was all by myself.

With my anxiety increasing by the second, I reached the door in record time. It was cracked slightly. Thank goodness someone had left it open.

"Hurry up, Cookie." Charlotte waved.

"You don't want someone to catch you sneaking in this way," Peggy said. "They'll think you're up to something suspicious."

Before I could answer the ghosts were gone. No longer were they behind me. Now I really was all alone out there. Peggy and Charlotte were already standing in the kitchen. No one other than the ghosts was in the room when I stepped inside. To my left were the large refrigerators and on the right were the grill and ovens. A large stainless steel prep island took up space in the middle of the room.

The kitchen led into another space that was mainly used for a buffet-style gathering or whatever random event they needed extra room for. There were no windows into this space, so with the lights off it was almost pitch-black. Thank goodness there was a sliver of light coming from the main theater area so that I could see my way across the room.

"I can't tell you how many times I roamed these rooms," Peggy said. "I used to scare people just so I'd have something to do. At least I had all the plays to watch."

"Yes, there is that," Charlotte said.

I made my way over to the entrance to the main theater. Voices carried from the main room. I wasn't sure how many people were in there. I wanted to get closer so I could make out exactly what they were saying.

"Maybe you can hide behind that stack of chairs in the corner of the room." Charlotte peeked out around the edge of the door.

"I think they'd still see me," I whispered.

"We can go listen in," Charlotte said. "We'll report back to you what is said."

"No offense, but you have a tendency to get things wrong when you listen in," I said.

She placed her hands on her hips. "I did okay last time, didn't I?"

"That was an exception to the rule."

"You two need to stop bickering . . . we have work to do," Peggy said.

"Peggy's right, we have work to do. On with the case," I said. "Now that you mention hiding, I wonder if the killer was hiding?"

"Why do you ask?" Charlotte peered around the corner again.

"Because Morris was a tall and large man. He would have fought whoever was trying to attack him. That means the person was probably hiding and jumped out to surprise him. The killer probably stabbed Morris before Morris even knew what hit him," I said.

"You have a good point," Charlotte said.

"So you think the killer was hiding somewhere near the stage?" Peggy asked.

"Yes, I think that's a good assumption. Now I need to figure out where," I said.

"Here's your chance, Cookie. The cast went around the curtain into the backstage area. Run out there and hide." Charlotte gestured with her hands.

Without thinking on it too much I sped toward the stage. Once in the middle of the room, I didn't know where to go. I stood there scanning the room like I was a lost child looking for my mommy.

"Do something," Charlotte yelled.

"She's like a deer caught in the headlights," Peggy said. "It's painful to watch."

"I told you she does things like this. You thought I was making it up. She drives me crazy." Charlotte gestured wildly with her hands.

Panic had set in. I didn't know which way to run. I needed to hide before the cast members came back. Ghosts yakking in my ears didn't help. I didn't want the cast members to know I was here. If they knew I was listening they might not talk as openly. I suppose I had gotten a reputation lately for being a bit nosy.

"Over there." Charlotte pointed. "Behind the curtain."

There was a small section of the curtain that rested against the wall. I raced over and climbed behind the fabric. It was just in time, too, because the cast members returned. My breathing was heavy. I hoped they didn't hear me. At least now I could hear everything that was said. Charlotte and Peggy stood next to me. I wasn't sure why they felt the need to hide behind the curtain too.

"It feels so creepy to be standing here where they found Morris," a woman said.

"Look out there and tell me who's talking," I whispered.

"No way. You didn't want my help before, so why should I help now?" Charlotte shook her finger at me.

"Are you really going to pout at a time like this? Fine, I'll look myself." I reached for the curtain but didn't grab it just yet. I'd give her time to change her mind.

Charlotte narrowed her eyes at me, but ultimately stuck her head out of the fabric. She didn't even pull it back. She peeked back in at me.

"I believe that woman's name is Rachel," Charlotte said with an attitude.

"There were a lot of strange things going on that day," the male voice said.

Charlotte poked her head out again for a

second and returned. "Brandon? Is that his name? He has dark hair."

I remembered fitting both of them for their costumes. At least now I knew who was talking. I hoped they would reveal more. An added bonus would be if it was something I hadn't uncovered yet.

"Like what kind of things? Other than murder," Rachel said.

"I saw Morris arguing with someone on his phone. That wasn't all either. I noticed James Chrisman hiding behind the curtain over here," Brandon said.

"Oh, he's pointing this way," Charlotte said with panic in her voice.

"What if they find you?" Peggy asked.

Was Peggy shaking? She seemed even more frightened than me. I froze, afraid to make a move. Would they notice I was hiding behind the curtain now? How would I explain that? And like Peggy said, would they find me? This was turning out to be a bad idea. Why did I listen to Charlotte? I hoped they didn't come over here to check. Could they see the outline of my body behind the fabric?

"That is odd. Why do you think he was hiding?" Rachel asked.

"Okay, they're not looking this way now. Whew." Charlotte pretended to wipe her brow.

"That was a close call," Peggy said.

"Your guess is as good as mine," Brandon said.

I hadn't expected to find out that James Chrisman had been hiding behind the curtain. That would have given him the perfect chance to jump out and attack Morris. It went right along with my theory. Had I discovered the killer? Eavesdropping was nerve-racking, but so far it had paid off.

I fanned my face. The heat was starting to get to me back here. Maybe a panic attack was setting in. I stared down at my white heels, hoping I could get out of there soon. That was when I noticed something on the floor right by my foot. Could I reach down and pick it up without being noticed? I wasn't sure I was that flexible, especially in a pencil skirt. I reached out and put my foot on the object.

"What are you covering up?" Charlotte narrowed her eyes. "Are you hiding something from us?"

"She does look suspicious," Peggy said.

"Why do you automatically think I'm up to no good?" I asked.

Charlotte pointed at my face. "Because you always get that wide-eyed look on your face when you're not being truthful."

I scoffed. "You're imagining things."

Charlotte tapped her foot against the floor. "Am I? Move your foot."

"I don't want to draw attention to the curtain," I whispered.

"That didn't stop you from moving your foot the first time," Peggy said.

"Fine." I shifted my foot to the side so that the button was visible. "Happy?"

"What is that?" Charlotte asked, leaning down.

I knew what it was. Even behind there where it was dark. I'd recognize that button anywhere. It had been on the sweater that Heather had worn. I'd picked it out for her. What was it doing back here? I was sure there was a reasonable explanation.

"It's a button," I said.

"Why were you hiding it? I know there's some reason by the look on your face." Charlotte pointed.

I would have to tell Charlotte the truth. An uneasy feeling settled in the pit of my stomach.

"It was the button from Heather's sweater," I said.

I felt Charlotte's stare fixed on me. Finally, I met her gaze. Why wasn't Charlotte saying anything?

"This isn't good. Why would the button be back here?" Peggy's eyes widened. "Unless Heather was hiding back here."

"I'm sure there's a good explanation for this," I whispered.

Charlotte lifted an eyebrow. "I certainly hope so."

We stood in silence as I contemplated my next move. Next, the worst thing happened. Something was tickling my nose. Probably the dust from the curtain. I wiggled my nose, trying to stop the tickle. It was no use. I held my finger under my nose, but the sneeze came out anyway.

"What was that?" Rachel asked.

"Oh, Cookie, I thought you were ready for prime time. This is a rooky mistake." Charlotte placed her hands over her eyes, as if she didn't want to see what happened next.

I couldn't help it if I had allergies.

"It sounded as if someone sneezed," Brandon said. "I thought we were alone in here."

"We are," Rachel said. "At least I thought so. Now I'm scared."

"I heard this theater was haunted," Brandon said.

"A ghost that sneezes?" Rachel asked.

Charlotte giggled. This was no laughing matter. Soon they would discover me behind the curtain.

"I have to do something before they find me," I whispered.

Charlotte pushed the hair from her shoulders. "Calm down, Cookie. Let the professional take care of this."

After Charlotte pushed her shoulders back she marched from behind the curtain.

"Where's she going?" Peggy asked.

"I'm afraid to find out," I said.

A loud bang sounded from across the room. Rachel screamed. Now my heart pounded. Was that Charlotte or had the killer returned?

"What was that?" Brandon asked.

"This place really is haunted." Rachel's voice was filled with fear.

Charlotte had done something. But what? What sounded like running echoed through the stage area followed by silence filling the space.

Charlotte popped back up. "Hurry up and get out of here before they come back."

I raced from behind the curtain and toward the back room. Charlotte had successfully chased them away. Charlotte wouldn't let me forget this. Now that she'd saved me from being caught she would remind me of this forever. She did deserve a thank-you. When I reached the back room I paused and leaned against the wall.

"That was a close one," I said, trying to catch my breath.

Charlotte quirked a perfectly sculpted eyebrow.

"Thank you, Charlotte. Without your help I would have been caught."

She studied my face to determine if I was being sincere.

"You're welcome," she said. "You have to admit it was kind of funny the way they ran away. Did you hear Rachel scream?"

"Charlotte Meadows, that's not nice," I said.

She stared at me. I bit back my laughter.

"Now what?" Peggy asked.

"I think it's time for me to get out of here." I rushed across the room toward the kitchen area.

Pausing briefly when I stepped inside the space, I scanned the room. When I realized no one was there, I raced for the door. I slipped out of the theater the same way I'd entered. No one knew I'd even been there. That eerie feeling returned as I hurried to the car. It felt as if someone was watching from the seclusion of the giant trees. A breeze swayed the branches; the only sound was the rustle of the leaves.

"I wonder if the killer slipped in and out of the theater just like this. Maybe he ran away into the woods after the crime," I said, pulling out the keys from my pocket.

"The police should check around for clues," Peggy said.

"Surely they have by now," Charlotte said. "Dylan should let you know what they found."

I rushed into the car. Branches moved even faster in the wind. Gray clouds were rolling in with an ominous-looking sky. At least I felt a bit safer in the confines of my trusty Buick. It was like a big metal hug. With the top down on the car that meant anyone could still get to me. I really was being paranoid. Luckily, no one jumped out from the woods to attack me. I cranked the engine and backed out of there.

Charlotte rested back against the seat. "Whew, Cookie, sometimes the things you get into."

I scoffed. "As if you don't love every minute of it."

Peggy leaned forward in the middle of the backseat. "This is fun. You two are a real hoot."

Chapter 11

Charlotte's Tips for a Fabulous Afterlife

Always look your best in case one of the ghost hunters comes around and snaps your photo.
There's nothing worse than a bad photo that will be passed around to every ghost enthusiast in the world.

Dylan and I had plans for this evening. He'd asked me to go on a picnic under the stars.

"How romantic," Charlotte said dreamily.

I decided on a simple black dress with spaghetti straps, a fitted waist, and a full skirt. Warmth from the sun still heated the night air, so the summer dress would be perfect. Plus, the full skirt would be comfortable as we sat in the park. My wedge heels were the perfect height for walking through the grass. The doorbell rang and I froze. Was it really Dylan this time?

"He's here!" Charlotte yelled. "Fix your hair, put on lipstick, do something."

She had popped out onto the front porch for a look. At least I had her to check for me now. I wished she'd been close enough to look the other night.

I frowned. "I already did all that."

Charlotte looked me up and down. "Oh, I suppose you have."

In fact when I answered the door, it truly was Dylan. He wore tan pants and a white button-down short-sleeve shirt. His face lit up when he smiled.

He leaned in and kissed me. "You look beautiful. Are you ready?"

I picked up my little black clutch from the table by the door. "All set. I'll be back later, Grandma."

Dylan frowned. What had I done? He didn't know about Wind Song and Grandma Pearl. Panic set in as I scrambled to think of something to say. As if I didn't appear wacky enough already, now I'd done this.

I chuckled. "Why did I say that? I guess I have my grandmother on my mind. I meant to say Wind Song."

Charlotte smacked her head. She probably would have preferred to smack my head. "Cookie, what have you done?"

"You should just tell him the truth," Peggy said.

He grinned as if he understood, but he probably thought it was another thing to add to my list of weird behavior.

"Close one, Cookie. You have to be more careful," Charlotte said as she walked along beside me. "Though I'm not sure he believes you. He's a detective, you know. He can sniff out a lie."

Apparently Charlotte and Peggy were coming along on the date tonight too.

"We can drive my car since it's such a beautiful night," I said.

"Great idea." Dylan opened the car door for me.

Dylan had a bashful smile at times. I loved that the vulnerable side of him slipped through on occasion. It didn't happen often. Most of the time he seemed calm and completely in control. I slid behind the wheel. With Dylan in the passenger seat and Charlotte and Peggy in the back, we took off. The park in the historic section of town would be mostly empty this time of night. The park wasn't the only empty thing around town. The streets were mostly empty too. This was just part of small-town life. I found a parking spot on the street by the front entrance. Once outside of the car, Dylan grabbed the basket from the trunk.

"I'm not sure you're supposed to be in the park after dark," Peggy said, looking around with wide eyes. "What if someone calls the police?"

Charlotte scoffed. "Dylan is with the police department so he knows if he's breaking the law, right, Cookie?"

Did they have to be so chatty while following us? Dylan knew ghosts followed me, but I didn't want to have conversations with them while on a date. A foundation occupied the middle of the park. Benches and picnic tables were scattered around the open space. The tall trees surrounding the open expanse made the space feel more secluded. There were oak, pine, and magnolia trees. Plus, the weeping willows' long branches waving in the wind practically called for us to sit next to them.

"How's this spot?" Dylan pointed.

"Perfect," I said as I peered up at the endless twinkling stars.

Dylan pulled out the blanket and spread it on the ground. Next, he placed the basket down and pulled out the contents.

"This is awfully romantic . . . it seems as if he's up to something." Charlotte stared at the scene.

After I sat on the blanket Dylan handed me a champagne glass. Charlotte screamed and I almost dropped the glass. The bubbling liquid splashed against the side of the glass.

"Is everything okay?" Dylan asked.

"He's going to propose," Charlotte screeched.

"This is exciting," Peggy said, popping her bubble gum.

They were completely overreacting, right? It was too soon to think about marriage, right? However, Dylan did have a strange look in his eyes. Why was he smiling at me like that? Now the ghosts had made me paranoid. Charlotte was good at that. The moon shone across his handsome face as he smiled at me.

Dylan finished his drink and set the glass down. He took my hand in his. "Cookie, there's something I wanted to ask you."

"Here it comes," Charlotte said.

"I don't think I can breathe," Peggy said, fanning herself.

"Of course you can't breathe, you're dead, silly." Charlotte rolled her eyes.

Suddenly my chest felt tight. Air wasn't filling into my lungs. Was I suffocating? Dylan didn't ask the question though. Instead he jumped up and took off running.

"Well, talk about cold feet," Charlotte said. "I thought he would at least ask first before running away. Maybe at the altar, but not now."

Dylan ran out the park gate and toward my car. I spotted a man running away. I jumped up and sprinted in that direction. Dylan chased after the man.

"What in the world is going on around here?" Charlotte asked.

"I knew we shouldn't be in the park this late," Peggy said.

I stopped on the sidewalk. After a few seconds, I spotted Dylan heading back.

"What happened?" I asked.

Dylan stopped in front of me. "Someone was messing around your car. I think he was trying to steal it."

"Good thing Dylan was here to stop him," Charlotte said. "Now he can get back to that question; although it kind of ruins the vibe."

"You saw him trying to steal it?" I asked.

"I'm pretty sure that's what he was going to do. Let me make sure your car is okay and that he didn't take anything." Dylan headed over to the Buick.

I didn't know what I would have done if someone had taken my car. That was my most prized possession. I stepped over to the Buick, almost afraid of what I'd see. As far as I could tell everything seemed fine.

Dylan pulled out his phone. "I just need to call this in."

The next thing I knew other officers had descended on the park area. Flashing blue lights lit up the night sky. I hoped no one passed by and saw me involved in yet another crime scene.

"This isn't romantic," Charlotte said.

No, it wasn't, but I had other things to worry about. Like someone stealing my car. Soon even more police cars arrived. Dylan talked with them while I watched from the sidewalk. I was on high alert looking for the person to return. I suppose now that the police were here he would stay away. What if he was hidden somewhere watching the scene? What if he'd wanted more than my car? Could it have been the person who left the note?

"How long is this going to take?" Charlotte paced across the sidewalk in front of me.

I couldn't answer because the other detectives might notice. Peggy fidgeted beside me. Clearly she wanted to wrap this up too. I was getting antsy from the ghosts' impatience. Plus the fact that a mysterious man had appeared to be messing around with my car.

Dylan stepped back over to me after speaking with the officers. They got in their cars. I assumed that meant this would all be over soon. I wasn't sure if I wanted to go back to the picnic now. I would be too worried about who was watching us or if the person would try something again.

"What do you think he was doing?" I asked. "Had he already gotten in the car?"

"It looked as if he was trying to get behind the wheel," Dylan said.

"He didn't have the key," I said.

"He wouldn't need one if he knows how to start it without a key," Dylan said.

"Okay, now that everything is settled down, I want to know what Dylan was going to ask you," Charlotte said. "Go back over there to the picnic."

The blue from the police car had faded now, leaving us once again in the dark.

Dylan caressed my arm. "You all right?"

"Just a little shocked."

"We didn't get a chance to eat the food," Dylan said.

"You know, after that excitement, I'm not sure I'm hungry. Maybe we should just leave," I said, glancing around at our dark surroundings.

"What? Don't be a wimp, Cookie," Charlotte said.

Peggy rubbed her arms, as if fighting off a chill. "It is kind of scary."

Dylan watched me. "Sure, it's been a stressful few days. I'll take you home."

Dylan rushed over and grabbed the picnic basket. While he was gone I kept an eye on my surroundings, just in case this guy decided to attempt an encore performance. After making the trip back through town and on to my house, Dylan walked me to the front door. I would have asked him to come inside for a bit, but it was getting late and I knew he had to work early in the morning. I kind of hated the thought of staying by myself at the house. Though I suppose having two ghosts and my grandmother the cat wasn't exactly alone. What if the person followed us home? Yeah, I was being too paranoid . . . or was I?

"Don't let him get out of here without finding out what he wanted to ask you," Charlotte said.

As I stood at the front door, I said, "There was something you wanted to ask me."

Charlotte and Peggy stepped closer so they could hear every word.

Dylan looked down at his feet. "I just wanted to ask if you would go to the department's award party with me?"

"That's it?" Charlotte tossed her hands up and disappeared through the front door.

Clearly she was disappointed. What had given her the idea Dylan was ready to ask me to marry him? She'd almost gotten me to believe it.

"I'd love to," I said.

Dylan kissed me good-bye and headed down the driveway in his police car. At least I was already inside with the door locked.

"He left his bag in the car."

I frowned. "What bag?"

"The one he carries with work stuff," Charlotte said.

"Why did he have that with him? How did I not see him with it?" I asked.

Charlotte shrugged. "He put it in the trunk when he put the picnic basket back there. I don't know how you didn't see it."

That was odd. Maybe Dylan hadn't meant to bring it along on our date.

"You should take a look at it," Charlotte said.

I waved my hands. "I can't do that. That's going through his things, and I will never do that. I'll give it to him in the morning."

Charlotte tapped her foot against the floor and crossed her arms in front of her chest. "At the very least you need to bring the bag inside. What if someone steals it from the car?"

Peggy's gum was stuck to the end of her finger as she gestured. "Charlotte's right."

"I'm always right, dear," Charlotte said with a big smile.

She had a point. Now I had to go back out there in the dark. What if the person had followed us and was lurking around? The same person who rang the doorbell and left the note? The one who had tried to get my car? Was this the same person responsible for all these things?

I sighed. "Fine."

I didn't bother to put my shoes on for the trip. My anxiety spiked as I opened the door and peeked outside. The silence was almost eerie. It was as if the sounds of nature were scared silent too. I was almost sure it was just my imagination, but it really felt as if someone was watching me.

"Are you going to stand there all night or are you going to walk to the car?" Charlotte tapped her foot against the floor.

"I don't see you going out there," I said.

With a blink of the eye Charlotte was outside by the car.

"Now get out here now." Charlotte pointed.

Peggy was now beside Charlotte. It looked as if I outnumbered. Wind Song meowed.

"Oh sure, take their side," I said. "It's easy for you all. You're already dead. Doesn't matter if there's a murderer out there."

"What can we say, we're lucky." Sarcasm dripped off Charlotte's words.

I released a deep breath and took off in a sprint for the car. I pulled up the heavy trunk and scooped up the bag.

"See, that wasn't so hard now was it?" Charlotte asked.

I slammed the trunk shut and raced toward the front door. That feeling of being watched didn't go away. Of course I hadn't expected it to either.

As soon as I crossed the door's threshold I stumbled over my own feet and fell face-first onto the floor. I groaned and looked around. The contents of Dylan's bag had scattered across the hardwood floor. I pushed up with my arms. Charlotte and Peggy stared at me with wide eyes.

"You're right, Charlotte, she is clumsy," Peggy said.

I managed to get myself up from the floor.

"What is all this?" Charlotte had moved closer to the bag.

I waved my arms as if that would shoo Charlotte away. "I don't know, but we're not going to look at it."

"It's kind of hard not to look now with everything out in the open like that." Charlotte leaned down for a closer look. "Oh, it's crime-scene photos from Morris's murder."

"Do they have photos of the body?" Peggy asked the morbid question.

"They have a picture of the murder weapon," Charlotte said.

"Will you two stop that?" I asked as I joined them next to the photos.

"It can't hurt to take a little peek," Peggy said. "After all the pictures are on the floor and you have to pick them up."

"You can't close your eyes while you do it," Charlotte said.

She was right about that.

"I suppose I can't help it if I see them by accident," I said.

"Now you're talking." Charlotte flashed a devilish smile.

"Though I doubt Dylan will believe that it was an accident," I said.

"Well, that's his problem." Charlotte placed her hands on her hips.

I reached down and picked up the photo of the knife used to kill Morris. I looked over my shoulder as if I was expecting Dylan to be back there giving me a disapproving stare. Instead, Wind Song was sitting behind me. She meowed. I wasn't sure if Grandma Pearl approved or not. Knowing her, she was probably all for it. I studied the photo.

"Well?" Charlotte said. "Can you make anything of it?"

"This knife is interesting. I've never seen one like it." I gestured toward the photo.

"Do you know a lot about knives?" Peggy asked.

Charlotte laughed. "Unless it has to do with fashion, then no, she doesn't know a thing about them."

"That doesn't mean I can't find out," I said.

"I don't think that will be easy," Charlotte said.

"I have to give it a try though. I mean, this knife has to be kind of unique. Where do they sell them? Are there a limited number? Maybe that would lead me to the killer."

Charlotte shrugged. "Perhaps."

She didn't sound convinced. I peeked at the other photos. It showed Morris, so I wasn't interested in looking any longer. I'd seen enough. Now I was reliving the instant I found Heather standing over the body. That wasn't something I wanted to remember. I gathered the photos up and stuffed them back into the bag.

"He'll never know you saw them," Charlotte said.

"I hope not, because I don't think he'd be happy if he knew that I had looked." I placed the bag on the table by the front door.

"It was an accident," Peggy said.

"Was it?" I raised an eyebrow.

"What is that supposed to mean?" Charlotte narrowed her eyes.

"Never mind that. It's getting late and I need

sleep. I have an estate sale in the morning." I headed for the bedroom.

Charlotte groaned like a teenager who'd just been asked to do their homework.

"Fine. You can sleep now, but tomorrow you have to find out more about that knife." Charlotte followed along behind me.

Peggy was on Charlotte's heels. It was like I was the conductor of a ghost train. After curling up under the covers I tried to doze off. After a few minutes of ghost chatter they finally quieted down. Charlotte was silent for the rest of the evening. She was probably pouting because of what Dylan asked. I was still worried about the person who had been messing around my car. Would they return to my house tonight? If they'd left the note, too, then it didn't look as if they would stop harassing me any time soon. They wouldn't stop until I stopped snooping around and trying to find the killer. Had Dylan seen the killer tonight when he'd seen the man by my car?

Chapter 12

Cookie's Savvy Tips for Vintage Shopping

─────────────

*Just because the person is working in the store
and offers advice doesn't mean
they know vintage clothing well.*

The next day, after dropping off Dylan's bag at the police department, the ghosts and I headed to the shop. Heather was still home in bed. I'd called to check on her. She promised she'd be in to her shop soon. Of course, I couldn't help but worry about her. The ghosts and I had already stopped at the estate sale. I'd actually found quite a few good items there. I was surprised to find a 1960s sleeveless white with orange and yellow tulip print Lilly Pulitzer dress. It had a full-length prairie-style skirt, and the neckline featured a collar with pleated lace. Also I'd scored a 1970s long-sleeved Geoffrey Beene white-and-red-striped shirt. The pin-tucked pleats on the front and fitted waist were the bee's knees. Now I was ready to get to work. I had a bunch of items to process and get out on the floor.

In the past few days I'd fallen behind with

work and I really needed to catch up. At least the ghosts understood that I had stuff to do this morning. Charlotte was always more interested in trying to solve the murder. I wanted to crack the case, too, but I also had my passion for vintage fashion. I hung a few dresses on mannequins and next I had to work on the front windows.

Charlotte was basking in the sunshine by the window when I moved to the front of the shop to work on the display. Summer was here and I had plans for making a bright and cheery scene. I was buttoning up a hand-sewn light mint–colored cotton crepe dress when movement caught my attention. A woman was walking past the shop. For a split second our eyes met. She looked away quickly. Where had I seen her before? Her long brown hair tumbled along her shoulders. The woman's haunting dark eyes looked as if she could stare a hole right through me.

"Did you see her?" Charlotte appeared next to me in the window.

If anyone saw me moving my lips they'd think I was talking to myself. At least I could act as if I was speaking to Wind Song. She had been asleep in the front window next to me while I worked. Now she'd woken up and was staring at the woman out on the sidewalk too. That meant Grandma Pearl was probably in control.

"That's Marie Damon." Peggy had moved

and was now standing to my right. "The one Morris was also seeing."

"How do you know?" I asked.

"I saw her at the theater. They came down to the costume room once. They were kissing so I took off and went upstairs."

"Are there any other secrets you're not telling me?" I asked.

Peggy furrowed her brow. "No, I think that's about it."

"Marie acted as if she knew you," Charlotte said. "Did you see the way she looked in here?"

"She probably saw me at the theater, but what is she doing here now? I need to talk to her, but what will I ask? It's not as if I can come right out and ask if she killed Morris."

"I'm sure you'll think of something." Charlotte sashayed away from the window.

"Why would she want to talk to me?" I asked.

"Here she comes back." Peggy pointed.

"You have to talk to her." Charlotte motioned toward the door.

"What would I say to her?" I asked.

"Maybe jump out there and tell her there's a sale," Charlotte said.

"Oh, that's not obvious." I placed the pants I'd been ready to put on the mannequin down and rushed over to the door.

I still had no idea what I would say to Marie. With my anxiety spiked I opened the door and stepped out onto the sidewalk. My gaze locked with Marie's right away.

"Don't panic, Cookie." Charlotte was right beside me. "Just act normal . . . wait, don't act your kind of normal; that might scare her away."

Charlotte always had the witty comments. It was too late for her less-than-sage advice. I had already freaked out. I had to say something.

"It's a beautiful day." I forced a smile.

Marie refused a smile in return. She didn't answer me either. Also, she kept walking.

Charlotte ran ahead and waved her arms in front of Marie. Of course Marie didn't notice. "Great job, Cookie. You're losing your chance."

I couldn't let Marie get away. I wouldn't give up that easily.

"Excuse me, but have I seen you somewhere before?" I asked.

Marie stopped and looked back at me. At least she had paused instead of walking faster. Maybe I wasn't so bad at this after all. The ghosts and I stared in anticipation. Would she answer?

Marie eyed me up and down. "I don't think so."

"Don't let her get away," Charlotte said.

I pointed. "Yes, now I remember. You were at the Sugar Creek Theater. See, I design the costumes for the production."

Marie's expression changed. She looked like a trapped animal.

"I don't know what you mean." The crease between Marie's brows deepened as she frowned.

"Oh, so she's going to play as if she has no clue. That screams guilty." Charlotte crossed her arms in front of her chest.

"I never liked her." Peggy eyed Marie up and down.

Well, she was having an affair with Morris and I was certain she didn't want anyone to know. That would explain why she would deny being there. Now I had to get her to admit to the affair.

"I saw you at the theater one day. You were friends with Morris." My gaze was locked on her.

There was no way she would get out of answering that question.

Her eyes narrowed. "We spoke on occasion."

"If by spoke you mean made out in the costume room like a couple of teenagers," Peggy said.

Charlotte laughed.

"It's a tragedy what happened," I said, shaking my head.

Morris had always been nice to me. He always had a smile on his face and a joke to tell. No matter what other people said about him.

"I have to go now." Marie turned on her heels and hurried away.

Charlotte's perfectly sculpted eyebrow lifted. "She's got guilty written all over her face."

"Not so fast, Sherlock." I held up my hand. "We can't accuse her of murder based on one conversation. Maybe she's just upset by what happened to Morris and doesn't want to talk."

"I'm with Charlotte," Peggy said. "Guilty. Let's go get her."

Charlotte smiled. "Thank you, Peggy. At least someone else around here is thinking rationally."

I rolled my eyes and headed back into the shop. "You call chasing her down the sidewalk rational?"

"Not chasing . . . merely following with concern," Charlotte said.

I went back to dressing the mannequin. Charlotte had other things in mind.

Charlotte leaned close to the cat. "Pearl, I bet you have something to say about that lady who just walked down the street. How about we get the Ouija board so you can tell us."

"She only talks when she's ready," I said, buttoning the shirt.

Wind Song meowed and jumped down from the window. She strolled over to the counter and jumped up. So Grandma Pearl was ready to talk after all.

Charlotte laughed. "Your grandmother enjoyed gossip just as much as I did."

I knew when I was outnumbered. If Grandma Pearl wanted to talk I was all for it. Though the last time had been a little scary. It was daylight now, though, and surely nothing spooky could happen. I pulled out the Ouija board and placed it on the counter in front of Grandma Pearl.

To strangers it would look as if I wanted a cat to play with the thing. For that reason I always made sure no one saw us. The only people who knew about this were Heather, Dylan, and the ghosts. And that was the way I wanted to keep it. Maybe Grandma Pearl really did have something to say about Marie. If Wind Song was taking over, though, she would just want to instruct me on what cat food to buy next.

"Is this Wind Song or Grandma Pearl talking?" I asked.

The cat stretched her long white paw and placed it on the planchette. We waited with bated breath. Grandma Pearl had become a lot better at using the board. I suppose she was getting the hang of it. She glided the planchette across the board with ease. The next thing we knew she had spelled out a word.

"*Floral*?" Charlotte repeated the word.

That was an odd choice.

"Anything else, Grandma?" I asked.

"Maybe she's talking about perfume," Peggy said.

Grandma Pearl moved the planchette again. This time she spelled the word *delivery*.

"A flower delivery?" Charlotte's eyes lit up. "Oh, maybe someone is sending you flowers? A secret admirer?"

How did Charlotte get secret admirer from that?

The bell above the door chimed and Wind

Song jumped down from the counter. Heather had just entered the shop. Wind Song strolled by her and over to the window to sleep again. Heather's shoulders were slumped. That was her permanent posture as of late. She shuffled over to the settee and plopped down. Dark circles lined Heather's eyes. She leaned back and released a deep breath.

"She's walking around like a chicken with an egg broke in it," Charlotte said.

"You would, too, if you were a murder suspect," I whispered.

"She looks like a zombie." Peggy pointed. "What was that zombie movie? Oh yeah, *Creature with the Atom Brain.* I saw that movie at the drive-in theater with my boyfriend. Oh hey! I remembered something."

I moved over to Heather. "How are you?"

Heather stared at me with her blank expression. "What does it matter?"

"Oh, this is worse than I thought," Charlotte said. "Tell her to suck it up, buttercup."

I wasn't sure now was the right time to relay that message.

"Are you opening your shop today?" I pushed Heather's hair away from her face.

Heather shook her head. I hated to see her like this. There had to be something more I could do.

"We're working on some leads." I smiled.

Heather just gave me a blank expression.

She stood from the settee. "I think I'll go for a walk."

We watched as she walked out the door and headed down the sidewalk.

"Well, that was depressing," Charlotte said.

"The poor thing," Peggy said.

"I've never seen her like that," I said.

Now more than ever I had to find the killer. Heather was acting as if her life were over. She'd done nothing wrong and I had to prove it. So far I had suspects, but nothing to connect one of them to the murder. I had to find out what the words *floral delivery* meant. Plus, find out about that knife. I had a long to-do list. Unfortunately, it would have to wait until I had a chance to leave the shop. My new part-time employee would be here in a bit. That would give me a chance to look into these clues. In the meantime, I had to finish the window.

Once Brianna was there to work I took off toward the diner for a quick bite.

"Where are we going next?" Charlotte asked. "Do you really think you should be eating here again?"

I cast a glance over at her. "I'm going to get a salad, for your information."

She scoffed. "If you say so."

I entered the diner and headed straight for the counter to place my order. Dixie spotted me and waved. I hoped that she would wait on me instead of Patricia. Actually, I didn't see

Patricia anywhere. A few seconds later Dixie
came over.

"What can I get for you, Cookie?" Dixie wiped
her hands on her apron.

"I'll take the apple and chicken salad," I said.
"Oh, and unsweetened tea."

Charlotte placed her hands on her head as if
she might faint. "Let's not get ridiculous now,
Cookie. I know I said watch what you eat, but
unsweetened tea is just offensive."

"Coming right up," Dixie said with a smile.

I was just glad that she had a few more healthy
choices on the menu. She had listened to me
and other Sugar Creek residents. While Dixie
handed the order back to the chef, she got
my tea.

She brought the to-go cup to me. "How's it
going today? Anything interesting?"

Peggy leaned against the counter. "I think she
means about the murder."

"Dixie loves to gossip," Charlotte said.

I unwrapped a straw and shoved it into the
cup. "There was one thing. I'm trying to find out
the significance of the words *floral* and *delivery*."

Dixie held up her finger. "Hold that thought."

She turned around to grab the salad. Next
she placed it in a bag with some of the vinai-
grette dressing I liked.

"She probably thinks you're crazy," Charlotte said.

Dixie leaned close across the counter. "Does this have to do with the murder investigation?"

"Yes, it does," I said, handing her the money for my order.

"Wish I could help more," Dixie said around a sigh.

I took the bag. "There was one other thing."

"What's that?" Dixie asked with wide eyes.

"Do you know Marie?"

Dixie's mouth dropped.

"What is it?" I asked.

"Marie works at the florist. She delivers the flowers." Dixie's voice was filled with excitement.

"Oh my gosh," Peggy said.

"Bingo," Charlotte said as she thrust her index finger in the air.

"Thank you, Dixie. You've helped more than you know."

"She didn't do that much," Charlotte said.

I had to get over to the flower shop.

"You'll let me know what happens?" Dixie asked as I turned to head outside.

"I sure will, Dixie. You're the best." I waved and headed out the door.

Naturally I was headed right over.

"Hey, what about me? I'm not too shabby with this detective stuff," Charlotte said as we walked along the sidewalk.

"Of course, Charlotte. Don't be jealous," I said.

"I'm never jealous," Charlotte said.

"Sometimes I think you are," Peggy said.

Charlotte narrowed her eyes at Peggy.

"Well, you are," Peggy added.

There was no time to eat my salad right now. That would have to wait until later. I had to check out that flower shop.

Chapter 13

Don't take things too seriously.
Things can change in the blink of an eye.
One second you're here and the next poof you're gone.

"The flower shop closes for lunch break soon," I whispered.

"You can't hide back there forever," Charlotte said.

If someone saw me hiding in the bushes they might call the police. What if Dylan was the one who showed up for the call of a possible burglar? It looked as if I was casing the joint. In reality, I was just trying to see if Marie really worked there. If she was inside I didn't want to go in and have an awkward encounter with her.

"Oh, the door just opened." Charlotte moved behind the big azalea bush with me, as if someone would see her too.

Would anyone ever see Charlotte other than me? It didn't look that way. I still didn't know why I was able to see the ghosts. I'd never had psychic ability in the past. Peggy had already been behind the bush with me. My guess was that sometimes the ghosts forgot that other people couldn't see them either.

"It's Marie," Peggy whispered.

Now my anxiety increased. I hoped Marie didn't notice me watching her. She paused for a second and looked around. Did she sense my stare? I held my breath, waiting for her to look my way. Instead, she continued down the sidewalk in the opposite direction. Thank goodness I'd gone unnoticed. She was holding a large bouquet of mixed flowers. Marie wore a shirt with the shop's logo on the breast pocket.

"It looks as if she really does work here. So that was what Grandma Pearl meant about the floral delivery," I said.

"But what about it?" Charlotte asked. "Just because Marie works here doesn't mean anything to the murder."

"I guess Grandma Pearl was just helping us find her. I wish I could go in there and ask someone about Marie."

"Why can't you?" Peggy asked.

"She can and she will," Charlotte said, trying to grab my arm.

She kept forgetting that her hand moved right through me. Or maybe she didn't forget and she just hoped that at some point it would work.

I frowned. "What do you mean can and will? Since when do you tell me what to do?"

"I don't tell you what to do, but I know your personality and you won't let a little nervousness stop you from going in there." Charlotte flashed a mischievous smile.

I peeked through a break in the branches. "You're right. I won't let that stop me."

"You won't let what stop you?" the male voice asked from behind me.

I jumped and fell forward into the bushes.

"Are you all right?" he asked.

When I managed to look around I saw Ken reaching down to help me up.

"Uh-oh," Charlotte said.

"This is awkward," Peggy said.

I took Ken's outstretched hand and broke free from the branches. His stare was focused on me as I ran through possible excuses in my mind. Unfortunately, I wasn't coming up with anything that sounded reasonable.

I brushed the needles from my clothing. "I'm fine."

Ken looked around. "Who are you talking to?"

"Ghosts." Charlotte laughed.

"I was on my phone." The words came out before I even thought about them.

"Nice try, Cookie, not the best excuse though," Charlotte said.

"I give it three out of five stars. Not a terrible attempt," Peggy said.

Were Charlotte and Peggy related? They

certainly acted alike. He looked down at my hands. Sure, I didn't have the phone in my hand, but I had to stick with the story.

"You might as well tell him what you found out. He is here to help you," Charlotte said.

"To be honest with you, I was thinking of going into the florist." I gestured over my shoulder.

"Buying flowers?" Ken asked with a smile.

"Only if I have to," I said.

He studied my face. "Why do you say that?"

"What I mean is I want to talk with the shop's owner. If I have to buy flowers to do that I will. Actually, it's probably best if I do."

"You're starting to ramble," Charlotte pointed out. "Get to the point."

"Is there something you found out?" Ken asked.

How would I tell him that my dead grandmother gave me the information? Technically, Dixie told me that Marie worked here. That sounded much better than a possessed cat.

I gestured toward the storefront. "I found out that Marie works here. I really want to ask her questions about her relationship with Morris."

"Now you just sound like a stalker." Charlotte stood beside Ken.

She eyed him up and down.

"I like his suit," Peggy said as she checked out Ken too.

"Have you tried talking to her?" Ken asked.

"Yes, she walked by the shop and I went out to talk with her. She wasn't exactly receptive to the conversation."

"You could have tried harder," Charlotte said.

"It was a weak attempt," Peggy said.

If only I could talk to those two right now. Their critique wasn't wanted or needed.

"So what's your plan?" Ken looked to his left as if he sensed Charlotte.

She batted her lashes and blew a kiss at him. Peggy giggled.

"That's where the flower shop owner comes into play. Maybe she would have information about Marie," I said.

"She'll probably be reluctant to discuss anything about one of her employees," Ken said.

"See, Ken is a smart guy." Charlotte wiggled her finger.

"You're probably right. If only there was another way," I said.

Ken smiled. "That doesn't mean you shouldn't try to talk with her."

"I like the way he thinks." Charlotte gestured.

"You should listen to him," Peggy said.

It wasn't like I had another option. It was talk to the owner or nothing. Plus it was kind of getting strange standing in the bushes.

"Would you like to come with me?" I asked.

Ken glanced over at the shop. "I guess I could do that."

The fact that he hesitated made me question doing this. Maybe it wasn't a good idea. Nevertheless, I would do it. Ken and I walked to the entrance. The ghosts followed along behind us. A mixture of floral scent hit me when I stepped inside. No one was in the room. Though a bell had chimed when we entered. I assumed someone would be out to help us soon.

A gray-haired woman stepped out from the back room. She was barely visible behind the forest of flowers. Soon she stepped around them and to the counter. She wore the same style shirt as Marie with the shop's logo on the front. Though her top was blue instead of Marie's red. Her gaze focused on Ken. She acted as if she recognized him. Did she know he was an attorney? Maybe she thought she was in trouble. I guess it was better than if I'd brought Dylan in with me. She would have thought she was being arrested.

"Welcome to the Petal Palace. May I help you?" She smiled while watching Ken.

"I'd like a dozen red roses please," Ken said.

I hadn't expected him to order flowers. Should I order flowers too?

"I'd like a dozen too," I said.

The woman eyed me as if she was a little surprised.

"Now you just look strange," Charlotte said.

I panicked. Maybe I shouldn't have ordered flowers too.

"Two dozen red roses coming up." She turned toward the cooler full of colorful blooming flowers.

Ken looked at me and smiled. I figured he wasn't totally put off by my ineptness. I moved closer to the counter, as if moving in on my prey. Okay, that was a bit dramatic, but I did feel a bit like a spy on a covert mission. She checked over her shoulder several times.

"This is such a lovely shop. Are you the owner?"

She looked back at us again, narrowing her eyes.

"She certainly is a suspicious one, isn't she?" Charlotte asked.

"She looks guilty of something," Peggy said.

"Yes, I'm the owner," she said.

I had to find out before I proceeded with more questions.

Our presence seemed to make her nervous. As she packaged the roses, I decided to use that time to ask questions. After all, it was the whole point of this trip. If I didn't act soon it would be too late. Soon she'd give us the roses and we'd have to leave. I loved flowers as much as the next girl, but looking at them after a failed mission would just be a sad reminder of my failure.

"I thought about having the roses delivered, but I wasn't sure if you have delivery service," I said.

Charlotte scoffed. "Subtle, Cookie. All florists have delivery."

The owner frowned. "Yes, we deliver."

"Do you deliver to the Sugar Creek Theater?" I asked.

"Another smooth question." Charlotte leaned against the counter.

"This is better than watching any play at the theater." Peggy stared with wide eyes.

Charlotte's commentary was making me nervous. I wasn't sure what questions to ask or how to broach the subject of Marie. I was doing the best I could. Ken could feel free to jump in and help at any time.

"Maybe Ken can save her," Peggy said.

Charlotte pointed. "Look at him. He's staring like a deer caught in the headlights. He's no help. Is this the way he acts in the courtroom? If so, Heather should consider new counsel."

That was easy for Charlotte to say . . . she didn't have to talk to this woman. It was stressful and I could totally understand if Ken was nervous. Charlotte could feel free to help any time she wanted to tell me what to ask.

The owner finished wrapping the roses, placed them in separate boxes, and put them on the counter. "Is that all?"

Her tone sounded as if she was ready to get rid of us. Actually it was more like she was telling us not to bother to ask for more. I wouldn't let her off that easily. I suppose I could come right out and ask about Marie. Though I doubt she would give an honest answer to a couple of strangers.

"I recognized someone I know who just left your shop. Does Marie work here? I know her from the Sugar Creek Theater. I'm doing the costumes for the production," I said with a smile.

"I suppose that's better, but still rather obvious," Charlotte said. "And I doubt you'll win her over with a dazzling smile."

The woman typed on the computer. "Your roses will be nineteen ninety-five."

Was she going to answer my question? I handed her my credit card and stared the whole time.

She scanned the card. "Yes, Marie works here."

Finally, an answer. Why did she seem reluctant to talk about Marie? She handed the card back to me and repeated the steps for Ken. When she was finished I figured I'd lost my opportunity to ask any more questions. Plus, I had a dozen roses. I suppose they would be a pretty addition to my shop. When I picked up the box the woman looked right at me.

"Marie made a delivery to the theater the other day." The woman had lowered her voice as if she was afraid of being overheard.

Was she trying to tell me that she was suspicious of Marie's trip to the theater?

"Did something happen during the delivery?" I pushed.

"Enjoy the flowers," the woman said with a forced smile.

"I think that means she's done talking to you," Charlotte said.

Ken opened his mouth to speak, but another customer entered, stopping him. I was glad that it wasn't Marie, but disappointed that I wouldn't be able to get this woman to talk more about what she'd just told me. Now I was even more nervous at the thought of being around her.

Ken touched my arm and motioned for us to leave. I suppose the conversation was over for the day. I held my roses in my arms and walked out with Ken. I foresaw more flower purchases in my future. We walked back over to the bush where I'd been hiding. It was kind of like our secret meeting spot where we could huddle and discuss the outcome. After all, if the woman saw us hanging around still she might call the police. Plus, Marie might return and see us.

Ken handed me the bouquet of roses that he'd bought. "These are for you."

I hugged the roses in my arms along with my bouquet. "For me?"

He flashed his gorgeous smile. "They'll look beautiful in your shop."

How did he know that was where I'd planned on putting them? I suppose it was an easy guess. Sometimes I could be so predictable.

"Oh, how sweet," Charlotte said.

"It's romantic," Peggy said, practically swooning.

It wasn't romantic. Ken was just being a nice friend, right?

Checking over toward the street I noticed Dylan's car at the red light. He was looking right at us.

Charlotte followed my stare. "Uh-oh."

How would I explain that Ken was giving me flowers? Plus we were hiding behind a large bush. I knew what it would look like to Dylan. I would have to just tell him the truth, but would he believe that? The light turned green and he took off.

"What do you think about what she said?" Ken asked, bringing me back to my current surroundings.

"She seemed nervous, right? Like she wanted to say more," I said, still distracted by seeing Dylan.

"Maybe she knew more," Ken said.

"I'll have to buy more flowers."

Ken smiled.

"It sounded as if she was hinting that Marie delivered flowers to the theater the day that Morris was murdered, but who received the delivery?"

"Maybe Morris was the recipient of the delivery. Only Marie was delivering a knife instead of flowers," Charlotte said.

"That's something we'll have to find out," Ken said.

"Thanks for the flowers," I said, gesturing toward the box.

Ken's gaze lingered on my face. "I should be going. We'll talk soon?"

"Yes, talk to you soon." I tossed my hand up in a wave.

Ken walked away and I headed for my car. Now I needed to call Dylan. I'd have to explain that it wasn't how it looked.

Chapter 14

Don't forget vintage clothing shops have clearance racks as well. You can find great bargains there.

While working with the vintage clothing was usually when my clearest thinking occurred. Hanging the clothing, sorting through it, and styling outfits were all therapeutic. So I wasn't too surprised when I remembered something I'd seen in one of the crime scene photos while styling a beautiful emerald-green Dior dress onto one of the mannequins in the shop.

"What's on your mind?" Charlotte asked as she sat on the settee watching me.

"There was a gum wrapper next to the body. What if the killer accidentally dropped it?" I asked.

"A wrapper? What if Morris was chewing gum?" Charlotte groaned. "I hate that smacking sound people make when they chew gum. It's gross."

Peggy popped another bubble and stared at Charlotte.

Charlotte shrugged. "Sorry, it's the truth."

"This clue could lead me to the killer," I said, checking the zipper on the dress.

"How would you possibly track down who left the wrapper?" Peggy asked between popping.

"Easy, I'll find out who chews gum." I strolled back over to the counter.

Charlotte and Peggy laughed at the same time.

"Why is that funny?" I asked.

Charlotte waved her arm for dramatic emphasis. "Just like that, huh? You'll find out who was chewing gum at the Sugar Creek Theater the day Morris was murdered. Even better, you'll find out who was right there at the crime scene chewing gum. It could have fallen out of someone's pocket days before the murder."

"Don't be logical and burst my bubble."

Peggy popped another bubble at that exact second.

"At least let me check. It'll make me feel as if I am making progress," I said.

"All I'll say is good luck with that," Charlotte said, giving a little salute.

I narrowed my eyes. "I'll show you."

I pulled out my notepad and pen so that I could take notes.

Charlotte leaned against the counter. "What are you doing?"

"Not that I should tell you, but I'm making a list of suspects so that I can check on each one. I will find out who likes to chew gum."

"I seriously think you've cracked this time," Charlotte said.

Peggy leaned closer so she could read my list. The whole time she was twisting the gum around her index finger before shoving it back into her mouth.

"Will you stop doing that? You're making me gag," Charlotte said, and scowled.

Peggy continued chewing, impervious to Charlotte's comment.

"So we have Marie, James Chrisman, Patricia his wife, and is there anyone else I'm missing?" I tapped the pen against my bottom lip.

"What if none of them is the killer?" Peggy asked.

"Then I have a problem," I said. "I guess I'd have to start looking for someone else. I refuse to give up."

Giving up on the list for the time being, I went about my day working. The ghosts were sitting on the settee as I sorted through a bunch of clothing I'd picked up at the estate sale. Peggy sighed, but I continued working. She exhaled again, even louder this time, and a couple seconds later she repeated the sound.

"I think she wants your attention," Charlotte said.

I put the dress down and focused on Peggy. "Is something wrong?"

She slumped her shoulders. "It's just that I've been thinking about my death. I know you've been busy with finding Morris's killer, but do you think there's any hope of finding out what happened to me."

Charlotte had told me to look into Peggy's death and I planned on it, but I guess I'd made Heather my priority. Now Peggy's sad face was heartbreaking.

I gathered up the rest of the clothing and placed it on the counter. "Brianna is supposed to be back in ten minutes. I suppose I could leave and do a little research about your death, Peggy."

She jumped up from the settee. "Really? Do you mean it?"

"Of course. Maybe I can look at the library and see if there's anything in the paper about your death."

"Honestly, Cookie, I can't believe it took you this long." Charlotte waggled her finger at me.

With a sinking feeling in my stomach I dialed Dylan's number. I'd been putting off the call. I should have done it right away. What would he say about what he'd seen? I knew what I'd think if the tables had been turned.

"Cookie Chanel, how are you?" Dylan asked.

Usually he didn't answer the phone by saying my whole name. That meant that he was definitely upset with me. Now what would I do? I didn't think Dylan had ever been upset with me. Not for anything other than telling me not to get involved with murder cases. After that I'd promptly proceed to ignore his request. I always had good intentions, though, so that counted for something.

"I was just calling to talk to you about earlier today," I said.

Charlotte and Peggy were clinging on to every word, as if watching their favorite television drama.

"What about today?" he asked.

He knew exactly what I meant, but he was going to make me come out with it. Okay, fair enough. It was the least I could do.

"Well, I know you saw me talking with Ken today, and he was giving me flowers, but it's definitely not as it seems." I rushed my words.

"How did it seem?" he asked.

Wow, he really was upset with me.

Charlotte studied the crimson-colored polish on her fingernails. "Well, at least you have Ken to date."

I brushed off Charlotte's comment. "Maybe there was a romantic gesture with the flowers."

"There's a romantic gesture with the flowers?" The tone of Dylan's voice changed, as if he was even more upset.

I could lie and say that there wasn't, but I had a suspicion that Ken wanted more of a romance between us.

"I suppose that maybe Ken would like to date me," I said.

"And what about you? How do you feel?" Dylan asked.

Dylan and I had been dating for a while, yet Dylan had always avoided the subject of Ken. It was odd, really. Now was finally the time when he'd ask. I knew it would happen sooner or later.

"Ken and I are friends. I consider him a dear friend," I said.

"I think you're avoiding the question, Cookie," Dylan said.

"I think so too," Charlotte said.

Did Charlotte and Peggy have to listen to every word of the conversation? I had to explain my feelings now, once and for all. But I couldn't admit to Dylan that I had thought of dating Ken in the past. That was when we first met, and I hadn't been exclusive with Dylan.

"I'm dating you now, and I hope that you feel confident with my feelings for you," I said.

"Just tell him you love him," Peggy said. "Trust me, sometimes it's too late to do those things."

She was right about that, but I was nervous to make that big step. What if he didn't tell me in return? Maybe he didn't have those feelings for me at all.

"So you see, the roses were nothing romantic."

Now I had to tell him the reason we had been at the flower shop in the first place.

"You see, Dylan, the reason we were there . . . well, it has to do with the florist. So we went in there, and of course, we had to buy flowers."

I chuckled, but Dylan didn't laugh in return.

"You could have told me about this and I would have gone to the florist. Why did you tell Ken and not me?"

"Oh, now he sounds mad," Charlotte said.

"I think it was a coincidence that Ken walked by and spotted me hiding in the bushes."

After a pause, Dylan said, "Okay, continue."

"Well, Ken didn't need his flowers, so he gave them to me."

"I thought I asked you to stay out of this investigation," Dylan said.

"People in hell want ice water too." Charlotte scoffed.

"Yes, you asked and I simply didn't listen," I said.

"Cookie, you're going to get yourself in trouble."

I knew I could avoid his questioning by using the same tactic I always played . . . changing the subject.

"Anyway, Marie delivered flowers to the theater that day. I think maybe we should check her out. She was inside the theater right before the murder."

"Okay, I'll check it out."

"He'll thank you for this lead later," Charlotte said.

I certainly hoped so.

"Stay out of trouble. I'll call you soon, okay, Cookie?"

At least he wasn't using my last name now.

"Now that wasn't so hard, was it?" Charlotte asked.

I waved off her comment and got back to work.

After Brianna arrived, the ghosts and I headed for the library. Wind Song stayed back at the shop. I wheeled into the library and found a parking space.

As we walked toward the entrance, Charlotte said, "I bet Dylan might be able to find some information about Peggy."

"Oh, I wouldn't want to bother him. He's too busy," Peggy said.

"Plus, he's probably mad at her for flirting with Ken in the bushes." Charlotte continued walking, looking straight ahead as she spoke.

"I was not flirting." I glared at her, but she didn't bother to look my way to notice.

I'd try to find details about Peggy first. If I had no luck maybe I'd casually mention it to Dylan. He wasn't angry with me. At least that was what he'd said. He had a lot on his plate, though, with finding Morris's killer. I hoped they really were looking for a killer. What if they were just focused on Heather and Dylan didn't have the heart to tell me?

We stepped inside the library and I paused. The space was large and I had no idea which way to head. I spotted the reference desk and figured I'd ask the librarian for help. They'd recently moved things around when they'd remodeled. It looked as if I might be the only patron in the place. Other than the ghosts I'd brought with me.

The middle-aged, dark-haired woman peered at me from over the top of her tiny reading glasses. "May I help you?"

"Where are the periodicals?" I asked.

She focused on her computer screen again and pointed. "Down the hall and to the left."

I stepped into the quiet room and headed over to an available microfiche machine. Okay, they were all available. I was the only one in the room. The silence was a bit spooky.

"Do you think you'll find anything?" Peggy asked, peering over my shoulder.

"I hope so," I said as I sat down.

I scanned through the papers for the year that Peggy had died. I stopped when I came to her obituary.

She leaned over my shoulder again. "Oh, that's me."

"Good catch," Charlotte said.

There was a picture of her looking exactly as she did today.

"What does it say?" Peggy asked.

"It lists her cause of death as undetermined," I said.

Peggy scrunched her brow. "That doesn't make sense. Why don't they know what happened to me?"

"Technically, there are ghosts who stay around because they were in an accident. They don't realize they're dead." Charlotte offered her expertise.

"That's not the case with me. I know I'm dead." Peggy paced across the floor.

"Maybe you have unfinished business." I glanced over my shoulder at her.

She tossed her hands up. "Wouldn't I know what that was?"

"Maybe you forgot," I said.

She released a deep breath and said, "Well, I hope I remember soon."

"What I'd like to know is what caused your death. What kind of injury. This doesn't say." I continued scrolling through the film.

"It looks as if you might have to ask Dylan for help," Charlotte said.

"I won't give up just yet," I said.

"I think that dress is somehow related to my death," Peggy said.

"A dress?" I asked. "What dress?"

"The one I can't stop thinking about," Peggy said around a sigh.

"The dress you're wearing?" Charlotte looked Peggy up and down.

"No, it's a special occasion dress." Peggy smirked, as if Charlotte should have known this little detail.

Charlotte's eyes widened. She wasn't accustomed to sass in return.

"Where is the dress? Was it in the trunk at the theater?" I asked.

"Yes, I think it's still there." Peggy twisted the bubble gum around her finger.

"Maybe we should go have another look at this dress," I said.

Charlotte lifted an eyebrow.

I knew that sounded crazy, but it was worth a shot. Besides, I needed to go to the theater and work on the costumes anyway. As much as I hated going in that building, I had to finish the job. The longer I stayed away from the theater the more it made Heather's guilt look more likely. I had to let people know that by me being at the theater I knew Heather was innocent. Never mind that I got goose bumps every time I thought about the place.

I pushed to my feet and headed out the door with the ghosts right behind me. The librarian eyed me as I walked by, but she didn't speak. I'd love to see her face if she'd seen the ghosts trailing along behind me. As I headed out of the building and hurried into the car, I couldn't shake the feeling that someone was watching me.

Chapter 15

Charlotte's Tips for a Fabulous Afterlife

Wear gorgeous shoes because your feet never hurt.
What's that saying?
The higher the heel the closer to heaven.

A short time later we arrived at the theater. Once again I parked in that back lot. It was just as spooky tonight as always. Dark clouds rolled in and settled over the once blue sky. The only sound was the chirp of insects and a hooting owl in the distance. Soon the thunder would boom and lightning would streak across the sky. Just what I needed, inside a spooky building with a thunderstorm outside.

"Are you going in?" Charlotte asked.

I scanned the surroundings. "Yes, of course, as soon as I get up enough nerve."

Inhaling a deep breath and blowing it out, I opened the car door. Once the door was open I had a short amount of time to get to the building's back door. It was like a race against time. Kind of like at night when you have to go to the bathroom but you don't want the monsters from under your bed to get you. Okay, I sounded like a four-year-old. Get yourself together, Cookie, I thought. I was a grown woman. I could handle this. Nevertheless, I hurried across the parking lot, not bothering to glance over my shoulder. If I didn't look that meant nothing back there could get me. I knew it didn't work that way, but wishful thinking, I suppose.

If the back door was locked I'd be in big trouble. I had no idea where Charlotte and Peggy were. I assumed they'd already passed through the closed door and were waiting for me. At least I hoped that was the case. What if they'd gone back to the car and left me all alone? Charlotte needed to open the door for me if it was locked, but like I said, she wasn't always the best at channeling energy to move things. Though she would claim she was the best. I yanked on the door and thank goodness it was unlocked.

I hurried inside the building. The kitchen was quiet and I assumed everyone was onstage practicing. I rushed through the room and over to the steps that led to the basement. Of course it was dark down there. I flipped the switch on the wall. The dim light came on, but it was little help. Why couldn't they add brighter lights down there? It was almost as if they wanted everyone to be afraid. Once at the end of the hall I reached the costume room. The room was a pitch-black void. Anyone could be hiding in there and I wouldn't see them. I eased into the room just a bit so that I could reach the light switch on the wall beside the door.

After fumbling for several seconds and starting to panic, I flipped the switch. The fluorescent light added an eerie glow across the room. It felt as if someone might be hiding behind any number of objects in the room. The mannequins always made me think I spotted someone out of the corner of my eye. I was definitely more afraid of the living than the ghosts.

"Where is the dress?" I asked Peggy.

"Over in the trunk." She pointed.

I rushed over to the trunk and popped open the lid. The beautiful clothing was just as I left it. Now to find the dress.

"There it is . . . the red one right there," Peggy said.

I pulled out the dress. "It is beautiful. I can see why it would be your favorite. I bet it looks gorgeous on you."

The halter-style dress had layers of red tulle around the skirt. It was cocktail length and had a silk sash around the waist.

Peggy stared at the dress as I held it up. "I just can't figure out what it is about it."

"Maybe it's just your favorite dress," I said.

She shook her head. "I think there's more to it than that."

"It's a dress. What could it possibly mean?" Charlotte asked.

"Oh, I know. Maybe someone gave it to you," I said.

Peggy nodded. "That's true, but sadly, I don't remember."

"Maybe it will come back to you." I placed the dress back on top of the trunk. "I hate to leave the dress in this trunk."

Charlotte eyed me disapprovingly. I knew what she was thinking. She thought I wanted the dress for myself. That wasn't the case. Sure, it was beautiful, but I didn't have to take all vintage pieces I found. If that was the case I would already have taken all the items in this trunk.

"I suppose I could take it back to the shop. Maybe if you see it more often it will trigger a memory," I said.

"Good idea," Peggy said.

Charlotte shook her head. "How sweet of you."

Voices carried down the hall to the costume room. I froze on the spot.

"Is someone coming?" Charlotte asked.

"It sounds like someone is coming down here," Peggy said.

Peggy and Charlotte went to the door and peered out.

"I don't see anyone," Charlotte said.

Another ghost? I hoped not, although that would be much better than a potential killer. The ghost of Morris would certainly help right about now. I gathered the dress and hurried

over to the door. No one was in the hall, but the
voices carried from somewhere nearby. People
were arguing, but I couldn't make out what was
said. I was almost afraid to find out. What if the
killer had come back to the theater?

I eased out of the room and down the hall.
I'd turned off the light in the costume room so
it wasn't as lit as before. Still I moved up the
stairs. The arguing had stopped, but the silence
was just as scary. I almost reached the top of the
stairs and paused. Anxiety pulsed through my
body. I tried to steady my breathing so I wouldn't
hyperventilate.

"We'll go look for you," Charlotte said, motioning to Peggy.

I was hoping they'd say that. Sometimes it was
nice having ghosts around.

"It's James Chrisman," Charlotte whispered
as if he'd hear her. "He's just standing out there,
but he looks mad. His fists are clenched like he
wants to punch someone."

I didn't want to be his punching bag. Now
what would I do? I didn't want to talk with him
right now. He'd know that I had overheard his
argument. Though I hadn't heard much of
what was said, and I didn't know who he'd been
arguing with. He wouldn't know that. I'd just
have to stand there until he left. How long
could he stay there? Didn't he have to get back
to the rehearsal? I shifted my foot and the stair
tread squeaked. I held my breath. There was no

way he hadn't heard that. Maybe he would think it was a mouse. Okay, that was wishful thinking.

"Oh no," Charlotte said.

"This is not good," Peggy said.

When I looked up, my gaze met with James. He was at the top of the steps staring right at me.

He narrowed his eyes. "What are you doing?"

"Act confident. Don't let him intimidate you," Charlotte said.

Easier said than done. His glaring dark eyes and clenched fists were kind of threatening.

"I'm working on costumes. It's my job," I said in a curt tone.

He eyed me up and down. Now I wondered if he was contemplating pushing me down the stairs. I'd tumble to the bottom and likely break my neck. It would look like nothing more than an accident.

"Maybe you need to get a different job that doesn't involve this theater," he said.

Now he was making me angry. Who did he think he was? Oh yeah, possibly the killer. I attempted to push back the fear and continued to stare right at him. Charlotte poked him. He frowned and looked around as if he'd felt it.

"Oh, I'd like to give him a good whack." Charlotte pumped her fist.

"We should smack him." Peggy waved her hand. "Or you should, Charlotte. I don't know how."

"If I see you here again things could get

ugly." He bent down and gave my shoulder a little nudge.

I wobbled a little but managed to remain upright and not fall backward to my death.

"Don't you touch her," Charlotte yelled.

James turned around and walked away, leaving me standing there stunned.

"Did he really just threaten you?" Charlotte stared in disbelief. "Are you okay, Cookie?"

A small gesture of my head was all I managed since I was still stunned speechless.

"You should tell Dylan," Peggy said. "I don't like that man."

I moved the rest of the way up the stairs. "Me either."

Staying away from the theater wasn't an option. Though I didn't want to run into James ever again. My life could be in danger if I did.

"Why does he want you to stay away?" Charlotte asked. "Unless he is guilty of something he doesn't want you to discover."

"He's definitely hiding something," I said. "And as violent as he seems it's likely he's capable of murder."

Once at the top of the steps, I peered around. I'd expected to see him waiting for me.

"I'm surprised he didn't try to escort you out of the building," Charlotte said.

Luckily for me, James was nowhere in sight. I needed to work on costumes, but right now I figured I'd get out of there. I headed toward the kitchen.

"Where are you going?" Charlotte asked.

"I'm leaving before James comes back to finish me off," I said.

"You're not going to let him intimidate you." Charlotte walked beside me.

"I'm not?" I asked. "Almost being pushed down the stairs was kind of terrifying. I don't want to go through that again. Do you want me to go through that again? Next time it might not end as well."

"No, of course I don't want you to be pushed, but you have to stand up to him."

"Charlotte, it's best if I leave for now. I'll tell Dylan about what happened. Maybe he can discuss this with James." I opened the kitchen door.

After a pause, she said, "Yes, I suppose that would be the best thing to do."

I stepped out into the back parking lot. As if things hadn't been spooky enough before, now I had to worry about if James would be waiting for me out here. He probably wanted to make sure I left. So far I didn't see him. I rushed toward the car, practically running. It didn't help that I couldn't see who might be hiding behind those giant trees surroundings the area.

"I've never seen Cookie move that fast," Charlotte said.

"Yes, and in those shoes too. Impressive," Peggy said.

Once I reached the car I jumped behind the steering wheel and cranked the engine. It roared to life. I could always count on my Buick. I backed out of the parking space and headed around the building to the front parking lot. As I drove by the front entrance, James was standing out there. I knew he would be watching for me. I guess he hadn't thought to look in the back. Lucky for me.

"Oh, look, there he is." Charlotte pointed.

"Don't even look his way, Cookie," Peggy said.

No worries with that. I punched the gas and got out of there as quickly as possible.

Chapter 16

Cookie's Savvy Tips for Vintage Shopping

─────────────────

*You don't have to wear vintage clothing.
Use it as art. Framing and hanging beautiful pieces
of clothing is a great way to decorate any room.*

The next day I had no choice but to go back to the theater. Dylan had stopped by the theater yesterday and had a talk with James. Of course he'd played it off as a joke and said I read too much into it. I knew differently. The cast needed the costumes finished, though, so I had to go back. I wouldn't let James intimidate me and make me stay away. Though I must confess if not for the costumes I would stay away to avoid the conflict. Luckily, this time I found a spot in the front lot, so I didn't have to park in the back where it was spooky.

The entire theater surroundings had a bit of a strange vibe, but it was far worse in the back. Not many cars filled the lot, so I was one of the first ones to arrive. I entered through the front door and hurried by the stage. Every time I looked over I had a flashback of the murder scene. I suppose that would always happen now.

I made it through the main area and to the back toward the stairs that led to the basement. No matter if the sun shone outside, none of that light made its way to this part of the theater.

Actually, there were only a few windows on the front of the building. No wonder this place seemed so spooky. I made it down the stairs and to the costume room. I flicked on the switch and headed over to the racks of clothing. Within a couple seconds footsteps echoed from outside in the hallway. I stopped on the spot. What if that was James coming to confront me again? He'd be even madder that I'd sent Dylan over to talk with him. Just as Charlotte moved over to the door to check it out, Jackie Anthony popped up. Her brown bob-styled hair framed her round face. She wore casual attire—jeans and a white T-shirt—for rehearsal.

"Did I startle you?" she asked.

I chuckled nervously. "No, I'm fine."

"It is spooky down here." Jackie peered around as she inched farther into the room.

She didn't know the half of it.

"I heard there are ghosts who live down here," Jackie said.

Charlotte and Peggy waved as they walked behind Jackie.

I laughed again. "Just rumors, I guess. I have your costume ready if you'd like to try it on now."

I pulled the outfit from the rack. Jackie took

the dress and walked over to the curtained area so she could change.

"Things have been crazy around here, huh?" she asked as she shimmied into the dress.

I was surprised that she'd brought up the subject. No one seemed to want to discuss it.

After putting her shoes back on in case I needed to hem the dress, she stepped out from behind the curtain and gestured toward the dress. "How does it look?"

"Fantastic." I adjusted the collar of her dress. "It has been difficult for my friend."

She looked down as if she wasn't sure what to say.

"Did you happen to see anything that day?" I asked.

Jackie was still staring down at her white sneakers.

"She's awfully interested in her tennies," Charlotte said.

"There was one thing that I thought was strange." She met my stare.

"What's that?" the ghosts and I asked in unison.

"I saw a woman leaving out the back door that day. It was right before everything happened with Morris."

"Who was it?" I asked.

Jackie shifted from one foot to the other. "I didn't see her face, just the back of her. At the time I didn't think much of it."

"Did you tell the police?" I pressed.

She shook her head. "No, I didn't think it was important."

Charlotte groaned. "Of course it's important."

"Every detail counts," Peggy said.

"What color hair did the woman have?" I asked.

"She had dark hair," Jackie said.

Of course with no other details the hair color wouldn't help me much. Though Marie had dark hair. Plus, she'd supposedly made a delivery that day. I would think if she left through this door maybe the police would get fingerprints. I wondered if she wore gloves since Dylan claimed there were no prints on the murder weapon.

"I guess I should tell the police about this," Jackie said.

"Don't worry about that. Cookie will take care of it for you," Charlotte said with a wink.

"I'm sure the detective would want to ask you a few questions." I cast a glance at Charlotte when Jackie wasn't looking.

Charlotte raised her eyebrows. "Well, it's true."

"I talked with them once," Jackie said.

Charlotte groaned. "Why didn't she tell them about the woman right away?"

The sound of footsteps grabbed our attention. Someone was walking slowly across the floor above us. It was as if they were trying to be sneaky. We paused and looked up at the ceiling as if that would reveal who was there. One step after another the person drew closer to the stairs.

Charlotte moved over to the door and peered out into the hallway again. "No one is out here."

"That was spooky. It was as if the person had vanished," Peggy said.

More than likely they were just waiting up there for us to come back up.

"I guess I should go now," Jackie said, grabbing her jeans and T-shirt and heading for the changing area.

Now I was worried about going back up there. Who might be lurking and waiting for us? Maybe Charlotte could go first and take a look around. Jackie came out of the dressing room and handed me the dress.

"You'll let me know if you think of anything else or maybe overhear any information?" I said.

She studied my face.

"I know my friend didn't do it," I said.

She inched closer to the door. "I promise I'll let you know."

Without another word Jackie left the room. I practically held my breath as she walked up the stairs. I worried that someone was waiting at the top for her. I shouldn't have let her go up there alone. Though she probably would have thought I was nuts if I told her about my concerns. Her footsteps echoed across the ceiling as she moved upstairs.

"I guess no one was waiting up there for her," Peggy said.

"That doesn't mean someone isn't waiting for Cookie." Charlotte raised her eyebrow.

She had a way of making my anxiety grow. I placed the dress back on the rack and started working on the other costumes. My mind just wasn't into it though. Usually I loved this kind of stuff, but the fear that someone might be up there waiting for me took all the pleasure out of it. After about thirty minutes I had to stop. At the very least I needed fresh air. I felt as if the walls were closing in on me.

I eased out into the hallway. With each step my nerves danced in my stomach like a 1950s sock hop. The trip up the stairs seemed to stretch out forever. I wasn't sure how much more my nerves could handle. I reached the top of the stairs and peeked around.

"I think it's safe, Cookie," Charlotte whispered, and motioned for me to continue.

I couldn't believe I was so scared now each time I came to the theater. I rushed through the kitchen and over to the door.

"You didn't park out there," Charlotte said.

"As much as I didn't like the spooky back parking lot, I thought it might be better than going through the main theater to the front lot. I can walk around the side of the building to the front," I said as I opened the door.

"If you say so," Charlotte said.

The ghosts followed me out. It was daylight, too, so that would make it less scary.

"I've never seen her move so quickly in those shoes," Charlotte said.

"She sets a new record every time she comes back here," Peggy said with a chuckle.

"Glad I can be the source of amusement for you all," I said.

I raced around the side of the building. To my right was the theater and on the left was a line of dense trees. The drive that led to the back lot was between them. I walked along that drive as I headed toward the front. A rustling noise caught my attention, and for a second I lost my breath. What had made the noise? An animal or a person? Was someone watching me?

"I told you walking out here wasn't a good idea," Charlotte said.

"Actually you didn't say that," I said.

"Oh well, I suppose I thought it."

"I thought it too," Peggy said.

"Don't stop, Cookie. Keep walking." Charlotte gestured.

I wasn't sure why I'd stopped. Just because I heard the noise? Charlotte was right. I should have done the opposite. Now I stood there as if I were frozen, staring into the wooded area.

"Are you waiting for something to get you?" Charlotte asked.

"No, absolutely not," I said.

Charlotte reached for me as if she could push me out of the way. "Get yourself into gear."

Thank goodness I snapped out of my trance. I hurried my steps and continued along the driveway. Every few seconds I checked to my left, hoping I wouldn't see something.

"Sometimes the things she does drive me bonkers." Charlotte was talking to Peggy as we walked.

"I can see where that would make you bananas," Peggy said.

"I heard that," I said.

"I wasn't trying to be quiet," Charlotte said.

Picking up the pace, I rushed toward my car and jumped in. Slamming the door, I shoved the lock down. I peered in the rearview mirror. In a flash I thought for sure I saw a person in the wooded area. Could my mind be playing tricks on me? With anxiety still coursing through my veins, I cranked the car and pulled away from the theater. There was no way I was going into the wooded area to check it out. What if someone really had been watching me? The thought sent a shiver down my spine. I didn't want to scare Charlotte and Peggy, so I didn't tell them about what I'd seen.

"So let's recap what we know so far," Charlotte said as she sat in the passenger seat of my Buick.

"Okay . . ." I said as I made a right turn.

My heart rate had once again returned to normal and I was no longer close to hyperventilating. Peggy leaned forward from the backseat, resting her forearms on the top of the front seat.

"What do we know so far? Marie was seen at the theater that day. She was having an affair with Morris," Charlotte said.

"Right, so is she guilty?" I asked.

"I'm not finished." Charlotte held her hand up. "James has threatened you and we know he had a fight with Morris."

"So James is the killer," I said.

Charlotte held her hand up. "I'm not finished. There's also Patricia Chrisman who is apparently extremely jealous."

"Plus, we heard her on the phone," Peggy added.

"So that gives her a motive for murder," I said.

"Yes, along with the others," Charlotte said.

"The list of suspects is getting long," Peggy said around a heavy sigh.

"We still have to figure out the clues. The gum wrapper at the scene of the crime and the knife used in the murder." I pulled up to the stop sign.

"Plus, Jackie said she saw a woman leaving at the time of the murder," Peggy said.

"That could have been Marie," Charlotte

said. "What if she used the delivery as an excuse to kill Morris? That was her reason for being at the theater. No one would question why she was there."

"I don't think this murder was planned. It was more of a heat-of-the-moment kind of thing," I said. "Since there were so many people around, if the killer had planned it wouldn't they have wanted to do it where they wouldn't be caught? The risk of being seen that day was high."

"True," Charlotte said. "But since she knew there was a risk of being seen she would just shrug it off and say she had a delivery."

"Who received the flower delivery?" Peggy asked.

"Good question. I have to find out," I said.

We rode in silence as we contemplated the murder. My cell rang, breaking my reverie.

"It's Ken," I said as I glanced down at my phone. "I wonder what he wants."

"Well, answer it and find out." Charlotte motioned.

"I don't like to talk on the phone while I'm driving."

"It's no different than talking to me now. Pick up the phone," Charlotte snapped.

Against my better judgment I pulled over to the side of the road and answered the call.

"Cookie, I need to talk with you," Ken said.

"This sounds important," Charlotte said.

I'd put the call on speaker. Charlotte always

gave me a hassle if I didn't. That was probably why she insisted I answer the call now so she could listen in.

"Is something wrong?" I asked.

I hoped that Heather was okay. Right away worry set in.

"Ken, I didn't expect to hear from you," I said.

"Cookie, I spoke with one of the detectives on this case. They're close to arresting Heather for the murder," Ken said.

"What? They can't do that," I said.

"They can and they will," Charlotte added to the conversation.

"Let's not panic. We'll figure this out." Ken tried to calm me with his soothing voice.

Unfortunately, this was one time that it probably wouldn't work.

"What should we do?" I asked.

Ken inhaled deeply and exhaled. "I really don't think there is anything we can do right now. Perhaps you can prepare her for this possibility."

"I think Heather has already resigned herself to the fact that she's going to prison," Charlotte said.

I didn't even like to hear such a thing. If there was any way possible, I would keep my best friend from being locked behind bars. She was innocent and I knew it.

"Thanks for letting me know, Ken," I said. "I'll find Heather and let her know."

"You're welcome. I would have called her, but I figured it was best if she got the news from you. I'll call as soon as I know something else," Ken said. "Oh, and tell Heather I'm doing all I can. Tell her not to panic."

"Fat chance of her not panicking. It's the pokey we're talking about, Cookie. Orange jumpsuits and cheap flip-flops." Charlotte shuttered at the thought.

"Oh, and let's not forget the disgusting food. I saw that in a picture show," Peggy said.

After hanging up, I released a deep breath and rested my head against the leather seat. I decided I couldn't tell Heather about this. Not yet. She would just worry, and there was nothing good that could come of that. She would be mad at me if she found out I'd known and not told her, but I was doing this for her own good. I pulled back onto the road with thoughts of Heather in prison swirling in my mind.

Chapter 17

Charlotte's Tips for a Fabulous Afterlife

White is nice for an outfit selection.
It goes well with clouds.
Unless of course you've been a bad person and are
headed in the wrong direction. Shame on you.

One of my favorite things was being in the shop and working with the clothing. Standing at the counter, I was hanging a navy blue with gold horse bit print silk Celine shirt. Charlotte and Peggy were at the counter with me. We'd been discussing clothing. A welcome break from the usual topic of murder. The conversation had tapered off and we were now enjoying the silence of the beautiful sunny morning.

"Now I remember," Peggy's voice echoed across the room.

Charlotte jumped. "For heaven's sake, don't scare me like that. At least ease into whatever you're going to say."

"Sorry," Peggy said. "It's just that I remember something."

"What's that?" I asked.

"I'm not from Sugar Creek. I didn't live here."

"That is interesting . . ."

"Where did you live?" Charlotte asked.

Peggy frowned. "I don't remember."

"How do you know that you didn't live here?" Charlotte placed her hands on her hips.

Peggy shrugged. "I just remember."

"What were you doing hanging around the theater?" Charlotte asked.

Peggy paced across the floor in front of the counter. "I don't know."

The silence returned as we contemplated what Peggy had just revealed. Wind Song sat in the window with her eyes closed. Her tail wagged, though, so I knew she was listening to the conversation. Apparently, she had nothing to add because she didn't jump down and join us at the counter.

I had a to-do list that involved the murder investigations. Next up on my list was to visit Morris's place of employment again. I wanted to ask the people who worked with him if they'd noticed anything unusual in the days leading up to his murder. Maybe I could go by there on my lunch break. Dylan had probably already talked with them, but maybe he'd missed something. Not saying he wasn't good at his job, but it was always good to have a second opinion. Though I probably wouldn't tell him I was going there. Some things were best left unspoken.

Peggy and Charlotte had moved over to the

settee to sit. Wind Song was still in the window. I was sewing a button on a light pink Bobbie Brooks cotton sundress. It had tiny pearl-colored buttons that ran down the front of the dress. With the full bodice, nipped waist, and full skirt the dress would look even cuter with a petticoat underneath. Add black and white saddle shoes with little white socks, and this outfit would be positively dreamy.

"Oh, now I remember." Peggy punctuated her sentence with a swift gesture of her index finger. She jumped from her seat and paced again.

Charlotte clutched her chest. "You did it again."

"Sorry," Peggy said sheepishly.

"What is it this time?" Charlotte asked.

"My boyfriend lived in Sugar Creek. That would explain why I was here."

I looked up from my sewing. "Now that is something. Do you remember any other details about him? Where did he live?"

Peggy sat back down on the settee. "I don't remember."

"Maybe it will come to you," I said.

"Just make sure if it does to tell us quietly." Charlotte fanned herself.

At twelve Brianna arrived, and I set out for Morris's former place of employment. I had a bit of anxiety about speaking with the people there. Maybe they wouldn't want to talk with me. The first time I'd gone to his office I had found a bit of information, and I was hoping to discover even more this time.

"I'm not sure this is a good idea," Charlotte said as we walked toward my car. "It's like beating a dead horse. You can't get blood out of a turnip."

"I get it, Charlotte, but it's too late because I already have plans to go. What harm can it do?" I asked.

Charlotte scoffed. "You never know . . . something could happen."

"Don't say such things," I said as I hurried down the sidewalk.

We slipped into the car and headed over to the building. Lunch hour traffic around Sugar Creek meant that the drive would take three minutes instead of two. The sunshine and a warm breeze made me wish the trip would take just a little longer. Or maybe it was my anxiety that made me want to delay the arrival as long as possible. I told myself I wanted to go, but the reality was I had reservations. Involving myself in a murder investigation was risky business.

"Okay, Cookie, I will allow you to go this time," Charlotte said.

"Gee, thanks, Charlotte." The sarcasm dripped from my words.

"But this time you have to ask some tough questions. Look the people in the eye and let them know you mean business." Charlotte pumped her fist.

"I'll keep that in mind," I said as I punched the gas to get through a yellow light.

At least the drive over was a pretty one. I tried to relax because I knew once I arrived that my anxiety would increase. I was on the cusp of a panic attack. Over the edge of that cliff were labored breathing, speeding heart rate, and dizziness. Followed by a trip to the emergency room. I didn't have time for that, so I would have to calm down. I turned up the radio, hoping that Elvis would help ease my fears. Unfortunately, even Elvis didn't help. We pulled up to the building and parked. I hadn't expected to see Dylan's car there. Sunshine glinted off the shiny chrome as the car sat by the front entrance. Now I really was panicking.

"Now what do we do?" I asked.

Charlotte tapped her fingers against the leather seat. "Good question. It seems we have a bit of a pickle on our hands."

I frowned. "A pickle on our hands? That doesn't help."

"I guess we should leave," Peggy said.

Charlotte scoffed. "Oh, that's not an option. What if Dylan saw her car? It'll be even harder to explain if she just takes off like that. I think she needs to wait until he comes outside and talk with him. Besides, Cookie was the one who insisted on coming here. She made her bed now she'll have to lie in it."

"Don't you think you're being kind of hard on me, Charlotte?" I asked.

"Just trying to make you tougher, Cookie."

"A tough Cookie." Peggy laughed. "Get it?"

Charlotte raised her eyebrow. "Oh, we get it."

"I can back out of here before he ever sees me." I clutched the steering wheel tight.

One bit of encouragement from Charlotte and I'd throw this car into reverse. Why was I ready to give up so easily? Charlotte was right. I needed to be tougher. Or a "tough Cookie" as Peggy said.

"Oh, I don't think that's a good idea. Trust me on this, Cookie. Have I ever steered you wrong?" Charlotte asked.

"As a matter of fact . . ."

She frowned. "Like when?"

"Like the time we broke into your house."

She waved her hand dismissively. "Yeah, but did you die?"

"Almost," I said.

Charlotte crossed her arms in front of her waist. "But did you die?"

"No," I begrudgingly admitted.

A smug smile spread across Charlotte's face. "Okay then. See, you should listen to me."

We could talk in circles all day if I'd allow her to. I needed to get back to the issue at hand.

I turned the key and shifted the car into reverse. "I think I should get out of here."

"Okay, but I'm telling you it's a bad idea." Charlotte tossed up her hands.

Charlotte always knew how to get to me.

I shut off the car once again. "Okay, I'll do it, but if this goes wrong, it's all your fault."

"I'll take that chance." Charlotte popped out of the car and Peggy followed her, leaving me alone in the car.

I suppose I could take off and leave them. That would only make things worse for me though. Charlotte would haunt me relentlessly. Plus, Charlotte was my friend, and I wouldn't do that to her, no matter how annoying she was sometimes. I opened the car door and eased out. My stomach was twisted into a knot. My stare was focused on the door, hoping Dylan wouldn't pop out.

"Dylan's not even out here . . . why are you sneaking around like a cat burglar?" Charlotte asked.

As I headed for the door, I spotted a man walking in my direction. He wasn't looking at me, but I panicked and hid behind a large shrub. It wasn't Dylan, but I didn't want to be seen by anyone.

"What is wrong with you?" Charlotte asked as she hunkered down behind the landscaping with me. "What is with you and bushes?"

Peggy squeezed in beside us. "Who are we hiding from this time?"

"I thought that man was coming over to ask why I was here. I panicked," I whispered.

"You need to calm down, Cookie," Peggy said. "This isn't good for your stress level."

"She's wound tighter than my grandpa's old watch," Charlotte said.

"Where is he?" I peeked between the branches. The fresh pine scent tickled my nose and I fought off a sneeze.

"I don't see him." Charlotte peered over the top.

"There he is." Peggy pointed.

The man had moved closer to the building. What was he doing?

"He's acting strange. Maybe it's a good idea that you hid," Charlotte said. "I can go over and see what he's up to."

"Wait," I said, grabbing at her arm as if that would stop her. "I want to move closer too. I think he's trying to look in Dylan's car."

"This guy could really be up to no good," Charlotte said. "Maybe you should keep your distance."

Now she wanted me to be cautious? She's the one who said I should get out of the car. I heard what Charlotte said, but I wasn't going to let that stop me from moving closer. Now that this guy was messing with Dylan, I wouldn't back down or let fear stop me. No one messed with the people I loved. There was another group of bushes. I just had to make it over there and I should be hidden from view again.

Dylan wouldn't be happy to find me taking cover in the shrubbery. I was doing this for him though. Surely he would understand. Dashing away from my hiding spot, I ran toward the other landscaping.

"Cookie, what are you doing?" Charlotte called out.

There was no time to slow down. The man could turn around and see me any moment.

Charlotte popped up in front of me. "Stop right there."

"Get out of my way, Charlotte," I said as I ran right through her.

I made it to the shrubs without being caught.

Charlotte huffed. "I can't believe you did that. I feel so violated."

"Maybe you'll learn to stay out of my way," I said.

"You're going to get caught," Charlotte said with a wave of her finger.

"You're just saying that because you're mad at me."

"I can't believe you ran right through her, Cookie. You two are crazy."

Charlotte smirked at Peggy. "I'll take that as a compliment."

The man looked in my direction.

"See, I told you." Charlotte smirked. "He's looking at you."

Thank goodness he only watched in my direction for a couple seconds and focused his attention on Dylan's car again.

"What is he up to?" I whispered.

"No good," Charlotte said in a disapproving tone.

Peggy pointed. "Look. He's chewing gum."

"A lot of people chew gum," I said. "But that is curious."

"It could be a coincidence . . ." Charlotte's sentence trailed off.

I suppose it was a bit suspicious, but I wouldn't convict him of murder based on a stick of gum. The man reached out and tried to open Dylan's car door. I should call Dylan and tell him to get out here right away. The man stepped back and removed his hat. Long dark hair tumbled to his shoulders.

"Whoa, I wasn't expecting that," Charlotte said.

"How did he get so much hair stuffed under that hat?" Peggy asked.

"Is he trying to disguise his identity?" I asked.

"If he is, then he just blew his cover," Charlotte said.

He ran his hand through his thick hair and placed the hat back on his head, stuffing the hair up underneath once again. I studied his face and noticed it.

"He has a scar on his cheek. Connor said Mike Harvey has a scar on his cheek."

"What would he be doing here?" Charlotte asked.

"That's a question I'd like answered," I said.

The man turned and walked away.

"I think we should follow him," Charlotte said.

"I don't know if following him is such a good idea," I said.

"I can guarantee that's not a good idea," the male voice said.

I screamed and spun around. Dylan raised an eyebrow.

"Oh, busted," Charlotte said with a click of her tongue.

"Uh-oh," Peggy said.

I felt the heat rush to my cheeks.

"Now you've got some explaining to do," Charlotte said.

I think she was secretly getting some pleasure out of this. There wasn't much explaining to do. Dylan was a smart man. It was kind of obvious what I was doing.

"What are you doing?" Dylan asked.

"That guy was snooping around your car." I gestured over my shoulder.

Dylan looked in that direction. "I don't see anyone. What did he look like?"

I pointed toward my head. "He has long dark

hair, but he was wearing it up in his hat. His name is Mike Harvey."

"And how do you know his name?" Dylan asked.

"That's a good question," I said with a nervous chuckle.

The ghosts had moved to Dylan's side and were now staring at me just like Dylan.

I frowned. "I talked with someone at Morris's work and the man gave me Mike Harvey's name. You should really check into this guy."

Dylan pulled out his notepad and jotted down what I assumed was the name. "I'll make sure to do that. In the meantime, you need to leave the investigation to me."

"Uh-oh," Charlotte said. "You tell him that simply isn't possible."

I think wording it differently would work better for me in this situation.

"Heather is in trouble. When my friend is in trouble I have to help." I searched his eyes, hoping he would understand.

He took my hand in his and walked me over to my car.

"You're being escorted off the premises," Charlotte said.

"Is he taking her to jail?" Peggy asked.

"Meet me at the diner?" Dylan asked.

"This sounds serious." Charlotte leaned against my car.

Normally, I would have said that leaning against my Buick was a no-no, but since she was a ghost there was no harm. I didn't want anyone to scratch the paint.

"Right now?" I asked.

"If that's okay with you?" Dylan flashed his lopsided grin that always made me swoon.

"I can do that."

"She's a sucker for that smile," Charlotte said.

"I can see that." Peggy chuckled.

He leaned down and kissed me and said, "I'll meet you there."

Chapter 18

Cookie's Savvy Tips for Vintage Shopping

*Don't forget to shop for vintage hats, gloves,
scarves, handbags, shoes, and jewelry.
There are a lot of fantastic pieces to be found.*

Sunshine shimmered across downtown Sugar Creek. A smudge of white fluffy clouds decorated the blue canvas of the sky. I found a parking spot close to the diner and hurried out of the car.

"This sounds serious. I wonder what he wants to talk about. He'd better not ask you to marry him in that greasy diner." Charlotte chatted the whole time we walked along the sidewalk. If I hadn't known better I'd say she'd had a lot of caffeine.

"He is not asking me to marry him," I said.

"Maybe not today," Peggy said.

The lingering smell of the grill greeted us when we stepped inside. I scanned the room and realized I'd beat Dylan here. The lunch crowd had already started to thin out. I slipped into a booth at the front of the diner. Dixie waved from behind the counter. After a few seconds, she came over and placed a menu in front of me. It was habit for her, but I didn't need to look at the menu. I had that thing memorized a long time ago, although occasionally she would surprise me by adding a new item or two.

"Just you today?" Dixie looked at the booth.

She was looking for the ghosts.

"Of course the ghosts are here. Dylan is on his way."

The words had no sooner left my lips than Dylan walked through the door.

Dixie smiled. "Good morning, Detective Valentine."

"Good to see you, Dixie." Dylan slid onto the booth across from me.

"I bet you'd like one of my new iced coffees," Dixie said.

"You have iced coffee now, Dixie?" I asked in shock.

"Sure do. How about two? It will help cool you off from this hot day we're about to have." She gestured toward the window.

"Sounds great," Dylan said.

"Two iced coffees coming up."

Dixie walked away and now it was just Dylan and me. Oh, and the ghosts. The spirits were always there. Charlotte would be upset if she knew I hadn't called her by name. She hated when I referred to her as a ghost. She said she was much more than that, which was true . . . but I digress. Dylan was staring at me with his gorgeous blue eyes.

"Apologize to him. Tell him you'll never do it again. Though we know it's not the truth, you can still at least tell him that." Charlotte nudged.

I couldn't lie to him. Charlotte was right about doing it again though. If it meant snooping around again to help Heather and find Morris's killer, I would do it. That was what friends were for. Helping each other and taking risks when they needed it the most.

"So should we talk about today?" Dylan asked.

I'd rather not talk about it, but I suppose a healthy relationship meant discussing things and being completely honest. Though I still wasn't being completely truthful with Dylan. I hadn't told him about Grandma Pearl. One crazy step at a time, I suppose.

I picked at the edge of my napkin. "Sorry about that. I'm only trying to help."

"By the time you're done with that napkin it will be shredded," Charlotte said.

Dylan took my hands in his. "I know you're only trying to help, but I just don't want you to get hurt."

"You'll check out that guy?" I asked. "Mike Harvey was his name."

Dylan nodded. "I'm working on it as we speak."

"Dylan is always on top of things. He really has his act together. I like that. However, so does Ken." Charlotte winked.

"How is that possible?" Peggy asked. "How

can he look into the guy so quickly? Does it have to do with those handheld gadgets you all have?"

She didn't get an answer though. Dylan moved on with the conversation. "There was something else I wanted to tell you."

"What's that?" Charlotte leaned close.

"Do tell . . ." Peggy placed her elbows on the table and propped her head in her hands.

Of course Dylan had no idea the ghosts were listening. He probably assumed I had ghosts hanging around, but he didn't always ask.

Dixie returned with our iced drinks. "So what will it be for lunch? How about a juicy cheese-burger?"

"I'd love one, Dixie," I said.

Charlotte turned to Peggy. "Normally, Cookie is indecisive. She's just trying to get Dixie out of here so Dylan can continue talking."

Peggy pointed. "Good idea, Cookie."

"Though I must warn you, Cookie, if you keep eating burgers you'll have a little too much butter on your biscuit. You want to fit into those pencil skirts, don't you?"

Charlotte and her advice. She drove me crazy.

"Great. What about you, Dylan?" Dixie asked.

Dixie hadn't let me finish. I wasn't turning down the burger because of what Charlotte said, either, although I was sure she would think that. Now this would only encourage her behavior.

I held up my hand. "I'd love one, Dixie, but instead I'll take the lunch salad with baked chicken. Light ranch on the side."

"Nice choice, Cookie," Charlotte said with a satisfied smile.

Dixie sighed. She offered salad on the menu, but I knew she thought my choice was boring.

"I'll take you up on that cheeseburger offer, Dixie," Dylan said with a smile.

She beamed as she gathered the menus. "A juicy burger coming right up." Her tone changed. "And a salad."

"Okay, now back to the important conversation," Charlotte said. "Ask him what he wanted to tell you."

"There was something you wanted to tell me?" I asked.

"Does he have a ring?" Peggy appeared next to Dylan, scanning all around him for a little jewelry box.

Charlotte had convinced Peggy that Dylan was going to ask me to marry him.

"I did some research to locate the ghost you told me about. The one from the theater." Dylan took a sip of water.

"Peggy," I said. "What did you find out?"

"I'm nervous." Peggy had stood from the booth and was now pacing next to the table.

"It'll be okay," Charlotte said.

"I found a missing person from 1956. She matches the description."

"Do you have a photo?" I asked.

Dixie brought the food, causing us to put a pause on the conversation.

"If he found me maybe this means we can solve what happened to me," Peggy said.

"Well, he is a detective," Charlotte said.

He reached into his shirt pocket and pulled out a folded piece of paper. My heart sped up as he unfolded the sheet.

Dylan placed the paper on the table in front of me. "Is this her?"

I peered down at the photo printed on the paper. Peggy's smiling face looked back at me.

From over my shoulder she gasped. "It's my graduation photo. I haven't seen that in years. How did he get that? He used that handheld device you all have, didn't he? That thing is like magic."

I met Dylan's stare. "That's Peggy. What happened to her?"

"It's still an unsolved case." Dylan folded the paper again and placed it back in his pocket.

"You mean they never found out what happened to me?" Peggy asked.

My stomach flipped. I had to tell Dylan that she was here now. "Peggy is sitting right behind me. She's leaning over the booth and talking about the photo."

Dylan's gaze traveled to the general area behind me. "She's here now?" he whispered.

I nodded. "Peggy and Charlotte are here."

Dylan grabbed a french fry and stuffed it into his mouth.

"He looks a little flummoxed," Charlotte said.

Once he swallowed, he said, "She doesn't remember what happened?"

"If I did I would certainly tell you," Peggy said.

I shook my head. "She doesn't remember."

"Her family reported her missing on May 20, 1956, at around three in the afternoon when she didn't return home."

"Where had she been?" I asked.

"She told them she was going for a job interview, but they weren't sure where. It wasn't in her hometown," Dylan said.

"Could it have been Sugar Creek?" I asked.

"It's possible. Her parents said in the report that her boyfriend lived in Sugar Creek. Perhaps she wanted to be closer to him," Dylan said, looking over my shoulder. "Does any of this ring a bell with her?"

Peggy plopped down on the seat behind her. "I remember my boyfriend. Like I said, he lived here in Sugar Creek."

"Yes, Peggy said her boyfriend lived in Sugar Creek." I relayed the information.

"What was his name?" Dylan asked.

I looked back at Peggy. She shook her head.

"I don't think she can remember that part yet. Maybe it will come back to her," I said.

"When they found her body they never determined a cause of death. I'll continue to look into it," Dylan said.

"Cookie will too," Charlotte said.

Just as Charlotte said, I would continue to check this lead out. Maybe the boyfriend was still in Sugar Creek. Or he had family around. I wanted to help Peggy all that I could. The subject changed as we finished our lunch. We discussed an upcoming event Dylan had for the police department and possibly taking a quick trip to the beach. My parents lived on Tybee Island. They would love if we came for a visit. My mother and I were complete opposites, but she was still my best friend. I would never tell Heather that, but our friendships were different. My parents adored Dylan. And Dylan didn't seem fazed by my mother's eccentricities. I suppose if he liked me it was just his way to like quirky.

After paying for the meal, Dylan and I stepped outside. Charlotte and Peggy were behind us.

"I should get back to work." I gestured.

"Me too." Dylan studied my face.

"Maybe now he will ask her to marry him," Peggy said.

I couldn't believe they were still thinking about that.

"I hope not. It needs to be somewhere romantic. When the time is right he will ask." Charlotte winked when I glanced over at her.

Dylan looked over his shoulder. He knew I was looking at the ghosts. Thank goodness he liked my oddities. I suppose we all had our quirks. Some more than others.

Dylan kissed me good-bye and said, "Stay out of trouble."

I flashed a smile. "Always."

He headed in the opposite direction, and I was going back to the shop.

"He doesn't seriously believe you, does he?" Charlotte asked.

"Probably not," I said.

"Now what can we do?" Charlotte asked.

"I think we should at least give it a few hours before we do anything to get into trouble," I said.

Chapter 19

Charlotte's Tips for a Fabulous Afterlife

*If you're going to attach yourself
to someone make sure you like her.
Otherwise haunting just gets tiresome.*

After waiting for a couple of cars to pass, I crossed the street and headed toward the Magic Marketplace.

"Are you sure we shouldn't get down to business right away?" Charlotte pressed.

"Like I said, we need to wait a bit before we get ourselves into another pickle."

"If you say so," Charlotte said around a sigh.

Peggy hurried along beside Charlotte. "Get into another pickle. That's a good one, Cookie."

I hadn't heard from Heather all day and I was beginning to worry. Was she avoiding me? Her shop looked open so I knew she was there. The smell of incense hit me when I stepped through the door. Heather was sitting behind the counter. She didn't even look over when I opened the door. Usually she greeted customers with her latest company slogan.

"She looks like someone stole her incense and Birkenstocks," Charlotte said. "Why so glum?"

I crossed the floor and stood in front of the counter. Heather continued to read her book. Dark circles ringed her eyes. Her hair looked as if she'd forgotten to brush it, and her white T-shirt appeared as if she'd grabbed it from the dirty laundry pile.

I waved my hands in front of her. "Hello?"

She snapped to attention. "Oh, hi, Cookie. I didn't see you standing there."

Charlotte leaned close and peered at the book. "*What to Do When Your Life Is Over.* Oh dear."

"That's sad," Peggy said.

I picked up the book. "You have to snap out of this."

"What's the point?" Heather stared at me. "I'm going to prison. My life *is* over. Someone will decide they hate me in prison and stab me with a shank. I'll never make it there. I'm not tough enough."

"This is one of the most pathetic displays I've ever witnessed," Charlotte said. "She's right, though, she'd never make it in prison. Cookie, you would probably survive. You've got a little more street smarts. Thanks to me."

I frowned at Charlotte.

She tossed her hands up. "What? It's true. Look at her all slumped over."

"Positive thinking will help." I patted Heather's arm.

"Here comes Cookie's cheerleader talk," Charlotte said.

I would ignore Charlotte's comments since Heather couldn't hear them.

"Cookie does always have a positive outlook, doesn't she? I could see where that would annoy some people," Peggy said.

I shot Peggy an unamused expression.

"Not me, of course. I love you, Cookie." She forced a cheesy smile onto her face.

Charlotte laughed.

"We're making progress on finding the killer," I said.

Heather perked up. "Oh yeah? What did you find?"

I exchanged a look with the ghosts. "Well, one of the cast members saw a woman leaving the theater, and I have a lead on a gum wrapper."

Heather slumped her shoulders and focused on the book again. "Thanks for your help, Cookie, but it's pointless. I doubt a gum wrapper will keep me out of prison."

"Way to make her feel better, Cookie," Charlotte said.

I hated to see Heather like this. The bell above

the door jangled, capturing our attention. Two women walked in.

"There's my appointment. I'll talk to you soon." Heather stood from her stool and shuffled over to the women.

"Wow, she's like a wet blanket. Wait until those women get a load of her glumness." Charlotte shook her head.

"It's depressing in here. And I'm dead. That's saying a lot," Peggy said.

I stepped out of Heather's shop headed toward my place. Just a ways down the sidewalk I spotted Patricia Chrisman.

"Look who it is," I said, pointing down the sidewalk.

"What is she doing?" Charlotte asked.

"It looks like she just left the hair salon," I said.

"We have to follow her." Charlotte motioned.

I picked up my pace so that I could catch up with Patricia. What I would do once I got closer, I wasn't sure. What if she realized I was following her? The ghosts and I hurried down the sidewalk.

"Move those short legs, Cookie." Charlotte waved for me to pick up the pace.

"There's only so much distance I can cover with this stride," I panted, trying to catch my breath.

Patricia had only taken a few steps when she

stopped. I almost fell over my own feet, I stopped so fast. I dashed behind one of the streetlights.

"That's not a great hiding spot," Charlotte said.

"It's all I have," I whispered. "It's better than her seeing me."

"I think she can still see your hips." Charlotte lifted an eyebrow, followed by looking me up and down.

I narrowed my eyes and sent invisible daggers Charlotte's way.

"What do you think she's doing?" I asked.

"She's getting something from her purse," Charlotte said.

"Oh no. Is it a gun?"

"No, it's not a gun. Calm down, Cookie."

I peeked out from around the light pole. Patricia hadn't looked back to see me yet. She was too focused on whatever she'd taken out of her purse. I couldn't tell what she was doing, because her back was facing me. She tossed something toward the trash and started walking again.

"Look at her. She just littered," Charlotte said. "How rude."

"Well, considering she could be a murderer, I guess littering is the least of our worries," I said.

"Don't let her get away." Charlotte pointed.

Hurrying out from behind the light, I raced

down the sidewalk. Once I reached the trash can, I stopped. I reached down and picked up the trash that Patricia had so carelessly tossed to the ground. It was as if she didn't care if she missed the trash can. Like Charlotte said, how rude.

I held up the silver foil paper. "It's the same brand as the one at the crime scene."

"How in the world can you remember that?" Charlotte frowned.

"Attention to detail, I guess."

Charlotte's eyes widened. "I think we have the smoking gun."

I wasn't sure I would say that, but this was certainly incriminating.

"That is amazing," Peggy said.

"What should I do now?" I scanned the street for any sign of Patricia.

She had disappeared around the corner.

"Walk down there and see if you spot her," Charlotte said.

I hurried down the sidewalk to the corner of the building. Not too fast because I didn't want to bring attention to myself. Though I didn't want to miss Patricia either. At the side of the building was a parking lot. Once I reached the corner, I peeked around the side of the brick building. There were quite a few cars parked in the small lot, but no sign of Patricia.

"She was probably parked here and left," I

said. "I guess I'll go back to the shop and call Dylan."

"Good idea," Charlotte said.

I couldn't help but feel kind of proud of my discovery. I felt as if I was really onto something. Sure it was just a gum wrapper, but this was better than nothing. It could actually lead to the killer. I peered down toward the parking lot for a few more seconds. I wished I could have caught up with her. Nevertheless, I had even more suspicions of Patricia now.

As soon as I had reached the shop and Brianna left, I pulled out my phone and dialed Dylan's number.

"I didn't expect to hear from you so soon," he said when he answered.

"I have something to show you." I knew I sounded as if someone had just chased me. This was exciting news for me though. I hoped he felt the same way.

"It sounds important," Dylan said.

"I found something that I think could potentially solve the case," I said in a rush.

"Are you at the shop?" he asked.

"Yes," I answered.

"I'll be right over."

It would be kind of embarrassing to reveal the gum wrapper to him, but I honestly thought this was something. I clicked off the call and looked at the time. I wondered how long it would take him to get here. I was anxious to get this out.

"You know a lot of people chew that gum." Peggy leaned against the counter and blew a bubble with her gum.

It popped and she continued chewing.

"What a way to burst her bubble," Charlotte said.

I slumped my shoulders. "She's right though. Maybe I shouldn't have gotten Dylan's hopes up."

"He probably doesn't expect much," Charlotte said.

I frowned. "Thanks for the confidence."

Charlotte shrugged. "Well, it's true."

I busied myself with folding clothes. Though I'd probably just have to redo them later. My anxiety was making me do a sloppy job. A few minutes later Dylan arrived. He hurried over to where I stood by the counter.

"What did you find?" That little frown line appeared between his eyes.

Nerves danced in my stomach.

"Well, you have to tell him," Charlotte urged.

I gathered my nerve and said, "When I was walking back to the shop I spotted Patricia."

"Yes?" he asked with interest.

I pulled out the little piece of foil paper. "She dropped this."

"This is cringe worthy," Charlotte said. "I want to cover my eyes and ears. Unfortunately, I can't do both at once."

"I can't watch," Peggy added, covering her eyes with her hands.

They were the ones who had encouraged me to call Dylan.

Dylan took the wrapper. "It's like the one in the crime scene photo."

I glanced at Charlotte and Peggy and gave them a smug look. Now it wasn't so embarrassing after all.

"Exactly," I said.

"He's good. I'll give him that," Charlotte said.

"Where did you find this?" Dylan frowned.

"Patricia tossed it in the general direction of the trash can outside. I picked it up."

"So we know she chews this type of gum. Without proof of her buying it this doesn't help us much."

"You tried, Cookie," Charlotte said as she sat on the settee.

"Better luck next time." Peggy sat beside Charlotte.

I wasn't giving up that easily.

"So what if I prove that she made a purchase?" I asked.

"That would be a lot of work." Dylan ran his hand through his hair.

"Yes, but if I get proof . . ."

Dylan released a deep breath and said, "Then, yes, if you get proof that would link her to the scene of the crime."

I smiled. "Consider it done."

"That is a lofty aspiration," Charlotte said. "But I have faith in you."

She should have faith in me, considering she was the one who had pushed me to get involved in the first place. Now I couldn't *not* be a part of this madness.

Dylan grinned. "Just be careful. What do you have in mind?"

"I plan to go to every store in town and ask if they have video of Patricia buying this gum."

His eyes widened. "That's a lot of work."

"I have to try," I said.

The bell over the door caught our attention. I was surprised to see Heather walk in. She still looked just as glum with slumped shoulders and a frown.

She shuffled over to the counter. "I saw Dylan's car out front and stopped by to ask him if he had any news. I'm sure he doesn't."

Heather sounded defeated. She didn't even look at us when she spoke.

"As a matter of fact I do have a new clue," I said.

"Is it that gum wrapper again?" Heather asked.

I frowned. "Yes, but this time it really is promising."

"So it's technically not a new clue since you already told me about it," Heather said.

Charlotte laughed. "She has a point."

"Heather, I know it probably doesn't seem as

if we are trying to find someone else to link to the crime, but I'm working on it. These things take time," Dylan said.

"Because you all think you have the killer already." Heather stared at Dylan.

I had to break up the tension in the room, which meant getting rid of Dylan for the time being.

"So I'll let you know if I find any more information about the wrapper." I gestured toward Heather with a tilt of my head.

Dylan nodded, taking my cue. "I'll just take this for safe keeping." He tucked the wrapper into his pocket. "I'll call you in a bit. Nice seeing you, Heather."

She tossed her hand up in a halfhearted wave.

"I don't think you're her favorite person right now, Dylan," Charlotte said.

Peggy waved her hands. "The tension in here is thick."

Dylan kissed me good-bye and headed for the door. He rubbed Wind Song on his way out.

"So what's this all about?" Heather asked when Dylan walked out. "What's so promising about the gum wrapper?"

"I just have to go to every store in town and ask if Patricia bought a certain kind of gum." I rearranged the necklaces by the counter, not looking at Heather. I knew how crazy this sounded. Sure, it was unlikely that I'd find the information I needed, but I had to give it a shot.

Heather stepped in front of me, so I couldn't avoid looking at her. Her eyes were wide. "That could take forever. What if she bought it somewhere else?"

"I have a feeling she didn't," I said.

"You know, now that I think of it, every time I saw her at the theater she was chewing that gum," Heather said. "She came to see Morris a lot."

"She must really love that stuff," Peggy said as she chewed her gum.

"Yes, imagine that." Charlotte rolled her eyes.

"As soon as I close the shop I will start my search," I said.

"May luck be on our side," Peggy said.

"We'll need it," Charlotte said.

Chapter 20

Cookie's Savvy Tips for Vintage Clothing Shopping

A damaged vintage item can still be used.
Maybe that great dress can be altered into a blouse,
or the fabulous shirt can be made into a scarf.
There are other uses for the vintage items
even if you think they are too far gone.
Don't be too quick to toss them.
Once the piece is gone you'll never get it back.

"We should have some kind of plan before you go willy-nilly around town asking people if Patricia Chrisman bought Wrigley's Spearmint Gum from their store. They'll think you're even crazier than they already do." Charlotte paced across the floor.

"Thank you, Charlotte. I'd forgotten how crazy I am. You hadn't reminded me in a few hours." I rolled my eyes.

"No time for sarcasm right now. We have work to do." She placed her hands on her hips.

I tapped my fingers against the counter. "Well, we can narrow it down to stores that are close by where she lives and works."

"That would make the most sense," Peggy said.

"Okay, good idea. That's a start," Charlotte said.

"Mr. Dierck's is the closest." I said.

"Let's roll." Charlotte motioned over her shoulder as she marched toward the door.

Peggy was right behind her with a bounce in her step. Her poodle skirt swayed with each step. What was I thinking? It really was crazy to think I could track down a killer with a gum wrapper. That wouldn't stop me from trying though.

We piled into my car and I pointed the Buick toward Mr. Dierck's Food Mart and Easy Gas. It was right around the corner from Patricia's house. I pulled into the parking lot and into a space up by the door. Lucky for me I was the only car in the lot. This would mean the attendant would have more time to speak with me.

"I hope Patricia doesn't stop in here while I'm inside asking about her." I glanced around at the empty parking lot.

"Don't worry. What are the odds that would happen?" Charlotte asked with a dismissive wave of her hand.

"With me? Pretty good." I got out of the car and walked inside the store.

The cool air circled me as I looked around. Aisles of miscellaneous items took up the space in the middle of the room. Coolers with drinks and other chilled items took up the outer walls. Mr. Dierck was behind the counter. I knew him because he used to play golf with my dad. I figured if I asked him not to mention this conversation to Patricia Chrisman he would agree since he liked my father. It would be a favor. Though he would probably tell my father. My dad would ask me not to get involved in a murder investigation. It wouldn't be the first time he'd made that request. He'd also say if I promised to stay out of it he wouldn't be forced to tell my mother. Heaven knew I didn't want my mother to find out. She'd be in the Prius and on her way to Sugar Creek faster than I could say *tofu.* Mr. Dierck stared at me as if he didn't know me. That was just his way though.

"Are you sure he knows you? He's looking at you suspiciously."

Once I reached the counter, he smiled. "Cookie, what a pleasant surprise. To what do I owe this honor?"

I smiled. "Good evening, Mr. Dierck. How are you?"

"Well, my golf game is bad, but other than that I can't complain." He offered a lopsided smile. The little wrinkles crinkled around his eyes.

"He knows you want something," Charlotte said from over my shoulder.

"Yes, I can see it in his face," Peggy chimed in.

"Listen, Mr. Dierck. I'm researching something and I wondered if I can ask you a question." I searched his eyes for a reaction. Any sign that he would be willing to help me.

His brow pinched together. "Sure, I'll try to help."

Whew. That was a step in the right direction. I'd been worried he would say no. Although I thought he would help, there was no way to know for sure until he confirmed it.

"Now let's see if he still wants to help after you ask him the crazy question about a gum wrapper," Charlotte said.

"Oh boy. It sounds wackier every time you mention it," Peggy added.

"Well, I know you have a lot of customers, but I wanted to know if you remember a specific one." Silently I said a little prayer that he would remember Patricia.

"This is a long shot," Charlotte said.

"I wouldn't bet on it," Peggy said.

I knew it was a long shot, but I was willing to give it a try.

"Unless the person is a regular I probably wouldn't," he said.

That was what I was afraid of. Nonetheless I pressed on with my question. I pulled out my phone. Patricia liked social media and had quite a few selfies on Instagram. It had been easy to find a photo of her. "This is the woman." I showed him the phone.

He moved his eyeglasses and peered at the picture on my phone. "Patricia. Yes, I know her. Lovely lady."

He wouldn't think she was lovely if I proved she was actually a killer.

"Well, I can't believe it." Charlotte tossed her hands up in the air.

"I'm shocked," Peggy said.

"When's the last time she came in?" I asked.

My anxiety increased as I waited for an answer.

He tapped his chin with his index finger. "I guess I saw her a couple days ago."

Would this be enough? After going to the trouble of tracking her down, would it just be dismissed? Just coming into the store meant nothing really. I had to prove that she had bought the gum.

"Do you happen to remember if she bought this gum?" I reached down and picked up a package from the display in front of the counter.

He gestured at the gum and said, "Yes, she always buys a package. That and a Diet Coke. How did you know?"

I guess he thought I'd just performed a neat trick. No neat tricks, just old-fashioned detective work.

"Now ask him about video," Charlotte said.

"This is getting real interesting," Peggy said with excitement in her voice.

"Would you happen to have that on video . . . you know, if the police asked for it?" I tried to sound casual, but this request was far from casual.

"You've really piqued his interest now," Charlotte said.

His eyes widened. "Yes, I could provide that, but is it a crime to buy gum?"

"It's a crime to murder someone," Charlotte quipped.

"Good one, Charlotte," Peggy said with a point of her index finger.

"Not a crime to buy the gum. This may lead to something much worse," I said, placing the package back on the display.

"Don't tell him too much," Charlotte said.

He eyed me and said, "I'll help if I can."

"He doesn't sound too thrilled about that," Peggy said.

"No one wants to be involved in a murder investigation," Charlotte said.

"Thanks for the information. If you see her will you keep this conversation just between us?" I asked.

"As far as I'm concerned this conversation never happened," he said with a wink.

"He's probably saying that because what you asked is so weird," Charlotte said.

Weird it was for sure, but I didn't care because I had my answer. I was one step closer to finding the killer. I turned and hurried out of the store before he asked me questions that I wouldn't want to answer. The ghosts and I piled into the car and pulled away from the store.

"I'm shocked that you were actually able to pull that off," Charlotte said. "I guess my skills are really starting to rub off on you."

"Did it ever occur to you that I'm a natural at this kind of stuff?" I pushed the brakes when the red light turned.

"I suppose you're not bad." Charlotte grinned.

As we sat at the red light I checked in the rearview mirror. "Does that woman in the car behind us look familiar?"

Charlotte and Peggy turned around for a look. The woman behind the wheel wore a giant straw hat and dark sunglasses.

"How in the world would you know? She's covered up like some kind of starlet trying to avoid the press," Charlotte said.

"That's what makes me suspicious. There's just something off about it."

"Well, there are a lot of wackadoos in the world." Charlotte swirled her index finger next to her temple.

The light turned green and I pushed the gas.

"I'm sure it's nothing to be worried about."

Charlotte dismissed my concern with a flick of her wrist.

Nonetheless, I kept glancing in the mirror, watching the woman. She stayed close to my car. A little too close for my liking. It was as if she was keeping pace with me on purpose.

Chapter 21

Charlotte's Tips for a Fabulous Afterlife

―――――――

Learn to use your energy wisely.
You don't want to waste moving an object
on the wrong person. What if you want to scare
someone and you just used all the saved up energy
on someone else. Again, choose wisely.

"She is riding your bumper like you're towing her car," Peggy said.

"Okay, so maybe it is something to be concerned about," Charlotte said. "What is her problem?"

"I don't know, but I need to get away from her." I made the next right turn and so did the woman.

"Drive to the police station." Charlotte pointed. "She won't follow you there."

"I don't think I necessarily believe that, but I'll do it anyway," I said.

"And punch it too. If the police stop you, fine, you can tell them a crazy woman is following you." Charlotte had shifted in the seat so she could get a better look at the car behind us.

"I wish we could get her license plate number," I said, hurrying through a yellow light.

Of course when I accelerated so did the woman in the black sedan. She had great driving skills, but I wasn't impressed. The street where the police station was located came into view.

"I wonder if she knows where you're going?" Peggy asked.

"Well, she's about to find out," Charlotte said.

I made the next right and whipped the car into the parking lot. Dylan's cruiser was parked in his usual spot. At least I needed to talk with him anyway. I'd tell him about what Mr. Dierck had said. The car sped past, but I noticed the woman looked my way.

"She's probably cursing you for doing that." Charlotte laughed. "Don't mess with Cookie, Charlotte, and Peggy."

"You outsmarted her," Peggy said.

Thank goodness that was over. Who was that woman and why had she been following me? Plus, I couldn't help but wonder if she would be waiting somewhere when I left the station. I'd have to go through that ordeal all over again. I pulled into the space and put the car in park. I released a deep breath and shut off the car.

"Now that I think about it, I don't think I'll tell Dylan about this just yet," I said with my hands still on the steering wheel.

"Normally I wouldn't agree with that, but I

think you're right," Charlotte said. "You have no proof that she was actually following you."

"Or even who she was," Peggy said.

"I do plan to get answers to those questions though," I said.

Of course I needed to tell Dylan what I'd found out from Mr. Dierck, but I thought it could wait until later this evening. There would be nothing he could do with that information right now.

Before Dylan caught me in the parking lot, I backed the car out and pulled onto the road. With my luck the woman would be waiting around the corner for me. I'd be on the lookout for that car again. As I headed toward the shop, the image of that woman behind the wheel of her car stayed in my mind. Why did she seem so familiar when I couldn't even see her face? It hit me . . . her hat. I knew they sold those hats in the boutique in town. That was why she seemed familiar. It wasn't her; it was the hat. Now if I only knew who owned one of those hats. It wasn't vintage, and I'd even thought of purchasing one for myself.

"What's on your mind, Cookie?" Charlotte asked. "I know when you get quiet that you're up to something."

I scoffed. "That's more like a description of your behavior than mine."

"Touché," Charlotte said with a click of her tongue.

I pulled up to the shop and cut the engine. "I recognized the hat that woman was wearing."

"You're really good with fashion," Peggy said, popping her gum.

"It's a natural talent," I said, taking the keys from the ignition.

"So what are you thinking? You couldn't possibly know who owns the hat," Charlotte said.

I tapped my fingers against the steering wheel. "No, but at least now I know why she seemed familiar."

"That helps," Peggy said.

I wouldn't be able to get this out of my head. After getting out of the car I headed into the shop to pick up Wind Song. As soon as I entered, Wind Song hopped down from the windowsill and ran over to the counter. She jumped up in one giant leap.

"I think she wants to tell you something," Charlotte said.

"It looks that way," I said.

Grandma Pearl had never seemed this eager before. That was if it was her talking and not actually the cat. Wind Song liked to think menu requests were urgent, and that was the only time she came through with a message.

"Do you want to use the Ouija board or tarot cards?" I asked.

"How will she answer if she doesn't have one of those?" Charlotte asked.

I pulled the board and cards from under the counter. "We'll just let her tell us."

"I can't wait to see what she has to say," Peggy said.

The cat moved in front of the board and sat down, stretching her paws forward.

"The Ouija board it is," I said.

"This is exciting." Peggy moved closer.

Wind Song placed her paw on the planchette. Soon enough I'd know whether it was the cat or my grandmother speaking. I hoped it was Grandma Pearl. With a delicate paw she moved the planchette around the board.

The first word came quickly and it left me speechless—*hat*. How did she know that someone wearing a hat followed me? That had to be what she'd meant, right? Grandma Pearl hadn't been with us. Was she really that psychic?

"I'm eager for the next word." Charlotte motioned for Grandma Pearl to continue.

There was no need in pushing her though. She was way more stubborn than Charlotte. The next word started with an *S*. She continued with a *U*, and more letters followed.

"This is a long word," Peggy said.

Midway through I realized what she was spelling.

"*Surveillance*," I said.

"Check the video," Charlotte said.

Grandma Pearl stopped using the board and I reached for my laptop. I'd recently installed new cameras that would allow me to watch what was going on inside and outside the shop.

"Oh, can't you hurry?" Charlotte motioned.

"It takes a bit to get to the screen." My hands were shaking from the anticipation.

After what seemed like an eternity but in reality was about a minute, I reached the time that Grandma Pearl would have been here alone.

"Look. Here comes someone." Charlotte pointed at the screen.

"She's wearing a hat." Peggy held her hand up to her mouth after speaking the sentence.

I couldn't believe what I was seeing either. The woman stepped up to the window and peered into the store. She moved over to the door and tried to open it. She was wearing the exact hat and sunglasses. Since the door was locked she went back to the window, peering in as if searching for someone.

"Maybe it's just a coincidence," Peggy said.

"I don't believe in coincidences," Charlotte said. "She's here for a reason, and she followed Cookie. I don't think she wants to find a piece of vintage clothing either."

As much as I hated to admit it, Charlotte was right. This woman gave me a bad feeling. Now I just needed to see her face so I'd know who I was dealing with. That was assuming that I would recognize her without sunglasses. If in fact it was Patricia or Marie, I'd recognize them right away.

"The woman is really tall," Peggy said. "How tall is Patricia?"

"I have no idea," I said. "Charlotte is five-seven. I'd say they're the same height."

"This person is taller than me." Charlotte pointed at the screen.

"So it can't be Patricia?" I asked. "Marie was even shorter, right?"

"Maybe one of them is wearing high heels," Peggy said.

Charlotte gasped and I clutched my chest. "What in the world is wrong with you?" Charlotte gestured and I followed her pointing finger. The woman with the hat was walking by the window. Why now? When she'd tried to get into the shop earlier, I was closed. Now that I was open she walked on by. This was too strange. Once at the other side of the shop, she stopped and looked my way.

"What do you think she'll do now?" Peggy asked.

She'd better not come in here and cause trouble." Charlotte pumped her fist.

The woman stepped away from the window and out of sight.

"You have to follow her." Charlotte gestured toward the door.

"I suppose you're right," I said.

Anxiety settled in my stomach like a heavy weight.

"Go, go, go," Charlotte ordered.

"Why don't you follow her?" I asked.

The little wrinkle that Charlotte hated formed between her brows. "I suppose I have to do everything around here."

She'd never let me forget this, but if this woman killed me on the sidewalk I'd never let Charlotte forget that. I rushed for the door and out onto the sidewalk. The ghosts were right beside me. My ghostly friends and I took off following the woman.

"It looks like this person is going back to the parking lot." Charlotte slowed down to keep up my pace.

"That was where Patricia parked before. I bet it's her," I said, trying to walk faster.

"Don't let her see you following her," Charlotte said.

"That's why you should have followed her instead of me."

"Do I have to do everything around here?" Charlotte tossed her hands up.

"You two need to quit arguing," Peggy said. "You're giving me a headache."

I was pretty sure Peggy had heard Charlotte say that. Peggy was picking up Charlotte's bad habits. We reached the end of the building. Around the corner was the parking area. I paused and slowly eased forward so that I could see down there. Charlotte and Peggy stood at the end of the building, not hiding behind the wall. They didn't need to conceal themselves behind a brick wall. The person had stopped by the car. It was the same car that had followed me. Now I knew for sure it was the same woman. Not that I'd had any doubt.

"I wish I could read the license plate. Why don't you go down there and read it?" I looked at Charlotte.

"Don't say that I don't help you," she warned.

Charlotte had only taken a few steps when I said, "Wait."

Charlotte stopped in her tracks.

The person took off the sunglasses.

"Now she's removing the hat," Peggy said. "It's like a striptease out here."

"It's not a she," Charlotte said.

"It's a man," Peggy said in a loud voice.

I couldn't believe my eyes. The person I'd thought was a she was in fact a he.

"I know who that is. Remember? That's Mike Harvey. He worked with Morris," I said. "He was looking in Dylan's car. Why was he following me?"

"Now we need to know why he's dressed like a woman and following you," Charlotte said.

His long hair looked like Patricia's. With the sunglasses, woman's clothing, and hat, I'd assumed the person was female. There had to be a reason why he was dressed like this. Did he do this all the time or was this so that no one would recognize him?

"This gets stranger by the minute," Peggy said.

"Welcome to Cookie's world," Charlotte said.

"What do I do now?" I asked.

"You should go over there and ask why he's following you," Charlotte said.

Yes, that would be Charlotte's advice. That was why I didn't always follow her guidance. She could get me into a real pickle that I wouldn't be able to escape.

"Since he could be the killer, I'm not sure it's a wise idea to confront him in a secluded alley-way," I said.

Charlotte frowned. "I suppose you're right."

Mike climbed into his car and turned on the engine. I wished I could have confronted him.

Chapter 22

Cookie's Savvy Tips for Vintage Clothing Shopping

———————

Depending on the piece of clothing you purchased, you might want to have a professional remove any stains you find. You don't want to chance causing irreversible damage to the great vintage find.

The following day while waiting for further information about Mike Harvey, I'd decided to track down some of Peggy's boyfriend's relatives. At least attempt to track them down. Someone related to him had to still be in town. If he'd been twenty at the time that meant he could still be living in town too.

"Peggy, do you remember your boyfriend's name yet?" I hoped she remembered.

I knew her memory was still spotty, but I crossed my fingers that she would remember today. A lot had been coming back to her in the last twenty-four hours. It was like someone had opened the floodgate to her memories.

"His name was Steve Walker." She spoke the name as if she had been waiting forever for me to ask. Her eyes widened. "I can't believe

I remembered. It just slipped right out like I'd always known."

Charlotte beamed. "I told you everything would eventually come back."

"I've been dead for years. Why did it take so long?"

"Probably because you had no one to talk to," Charlotte said.

"So Cookie is the reason?" She stepped closer to me. "I wish I could hug you. Thank you."

"Don't thank me. Thank whatever or whoever gave me this ability to see ghosts. I still don't know why it happened," I said.

"Well, until you find out I will just have to thank you," Peggy said.

At least I had a name now. I'd hoped for a less common name so the search would be easier. What if I found multiple Steve Walkers in Sugar Creek?

"What are you up to?" Charlotte asked while peeking over my shoulder.

I'd turned on my computer. "I'm going to search this ancestry site and see if anyone lists his name."

"Why not just search his name?" Charlotte asked.

"I suppose that would be the best way to start." I typed the name into the search engine with Sugar Creek as well.

"What did you find?" Peggy asked with excitement in her voice.

"I'm surprised, but I actually found an address for a Steve Walker. Don't get too excited though. This might not be the right Steve Walker."

"See, I told you to look for his name first," Charlotte said.

"Yes, but is this information accurate? I guess we'll have to go there and find out." I shut off the computer.

"You mean I might actually see him again? I'm nervous." Peggy's voice wavered.

"Nothing to be nervous about," Charlotte said.

"Just remember he will look different than he did in the fifties. It's been sixty years. He's not a young adult anymore," I said.

Peggy pushed her shoulders back and stood a little straighter. "I understand."

I knew she'd agreed, but it would still be a bit of a shock for her.

After Brianna showed up for work we piled into my car and headed over to the address listed for Steve Walker. The small ranch-style brick house was located on a quiet cul-de-sac. Tall trees lined the streets and colorful flowers popped along the backdrop of the homes. I pulled up in front along the curb and cut the engine. Peggy remained silent as she peered out the window.

"I wonder if he lives here alone?" Charlotte asked.

What if he'd lived his life mourning for Peggy

and remained alone in that small house? She was acting surprisingly calm. I figured I was more nervous than she was based on how relaxed she seemed. Back at the shop she'd been fidgeting. Now she stayed perfectly still as she peered out the car window. Almost as if she were in a trance. Maybe she was in shock.

I opened the car door. "I suppose I should get to it."

Charlotte got out of the car, but Peggy remained in the backseat.

"Uh-oh," Charlotte said.

"We shouldn't make her go if she doesn't want to," I whispered.

Leaving Peggy in the car, Charlotte and I walked up the path to the front door. I glanced back to see that Peggy was standing right behind me. I smiled. It would be hard for her, but she'd found the courage to see him. After ringing the doorbell someone opened the door. A petite woman in her early thirties with dark hair answered.

"My name is Cookie and this is . . ." Oops. I'd almost introduced Charlotte.

"Watch what you're doing, Cookie," Charlotte said.

"Uh, I'm looking for Steve Walker."

"That was my uncle. He passed away about six months ago." She searched my face, clearly intrigued as to why I was asking.

"I'm sorry to hear that."

When I checked over my shoulder I realized Peggy was back at the car. I guess she didn't want to listen after hearing the sad news. That was completely understandable. Charlotte was still beside me.

"Is there something I can help you with?" the woman asked.

"You'd better hurry up, Cookie; I think this woman is losing her patience. She'll probably close the door soon," Charlotte said.

She seemed fine to me. Curious, but fine. Regardless, I'd do as Charlotte suggested.

"Do you know if your uncle had any connection with the Sugar Creek Theater?"

She frowned. "Yes, he worked there for a number of years."

"Well, that would explain why Peggy might be there," Charlotte said.

That was an interesting turn of events. I had to press for more answers.

"Do you know a woman named Peggy Page? He might have been friends with her back in the fifties?" I asked.

She shook her head. "He never mentioned anyone by that name. Is there some reason you are looking for him?"

I hadn't planned for that question. I should have, though, because it would be natural for her to ask. Now my anxiety had increased. The more nervous I became the more suspicious I would sound.

"You'd better say something fast. And make it good," Charlotte said.

Charlotte always told me what to do, but rarely offered suggestions on what to say.

"I'm working on costumes for the theater and found a piece of paper with your uncle's name on it in the basement. Peggy's name was on it as well. I was just curious about the history of the theater."

Charlotte held her hand up to her forehead as if she might faint. "Cookie, you should stop talking now because nothing you're saying is making any sense. That sounds like a made-up story."

Charlotte was being overly dramatic. I thought the story sounded completely plausible and that the woman would totally believe me.

The woman's brow pinched together. "What was the paper?"

Okay, maybe I had been wrong. She did look suspicious after all. That thing about my nerves making me sound suspect was right. What would I say now? I had to think of something. My mind was blank.

"Oh, it was just his name," I said nervously.

I'd tried to hide my apprehension, but it wasn't working. Perhaps it was time for me to get out of there.

She eyed me up and down.

"Don't just stand there with your eyes bugged out. Tell her you have to leave now," Charlotte said.

"Well, anyway, thanks for the help." I turned and hurried away from the house.

"You're not good under pressure, are you?" Charlotte asked as we hurried to the car.

"Is she still watching me?" I asked.

Charlotte looked over her shoulder. "Yes."

Peggy was already in the backseat. She'd been leaning against the car until she'd seen Charlotte and me rushing toward her. I suppose she figured out we were trying to make a quick getaway. Releasing a breath of relief, I slipped behind the wheel and cranked the engine. The woman watched as I pulled away from the curb.

Charlotte brushed the hair out of her eyes. "The things you get me into."

I wouldn't even respond to that. It was the other way around. Charlotte was the one getting me into trouble.

"Whew. I'm glad to be out of there." I peeked in the rearview mirror.

Peggy had a stunned look on her face. "Now I remember."

"Remember what?" I asked.

"I was at the theater with Steve," Peggy said.

Charlotte looked back at Peggy. "What happened?"

Peggy frowned. "That part I can't remember.

It's something, though, right? I mean, at least I remember that I was actually there."

I stopped at the red light. We had almost arrived back at my shop. "Yes, that is something. Maybe more will come back to you."

"We could try to do something to spark your memory," Charlotte said.

"Like what?" Peggy asked.

"Going back to the theater would be a start," I said.

"I don't know. She was there for years and nothing came back to her," Charlotte said.

"Good point," I said. "Nevertheless, now that this memory has returned, it wouldn't hurt to give it a try."

"I'm willing to give it a try," Peggy said.

"I suppose I do need to go back and finish up a few things with the costumes anyway."

I'd been putting it off because every time I thought of the theater my anxiety increased.

As I pulled up to the shop, I spotted Heather coming out of her place. She locked the door and headed down the street without even looking in my direction.

"I suppose she didn't see me," I said as I cut the ignition.

"Yes, I guess that's it," Charlotte said with doubt in her voice.

I got out of the car and rushed down the sidewalk to catch up to her. "Heather, you're leaving early. Is everything okay?"

She didn't look over at me as she kept on walking. "Cookie, save yourself. Don't even talk to me."

"What are you talking about?" I asked, trying to keep up.

Her legs were much longer than mine.

"Looks like she doesn't want to talk with you," Charlotte said.

"Yes, take a hint, Cookie," Peggy added.

"Can you slow the pace there? I feel like I'm in a marathon," I said through my heavy breathing.

"I'm leaving Sugar Creek, Cookie. I'll try to be in touch, but I can't guarantee anything." Heather stared straight ahead.

"What? Have you lost your mind?" I asked.

"Cookie, I thought we established this a long time ago?" Charlotte smirked.

I glared at Charlotte. This was no time for jokes. I jumped in front of Heather, forcing her to stop or run into me. Thank goodness because I was getting a serious cardio session from trying to keep up.

"I'm going to miss you so much. If I look at you I'll start crying. I probably won't be able to go through with it. That's why I was trying to get out of here before you came back." She wiped her cheek with the back of her hand.

"It's like she's going into the witness protection program," Charlotte said.

"This is not a good idea," I said. "It won't

work. You can't run. They'll definitely think you're guilty."

"It can't get any worse," Heather said. "At least I won't be in prison."

"They will think you're guilty," I repeated.

I touched her arms and she finally looked at me. Her green eyes shimmered from the watery tears. I hated to see her like this.

Heather blew the bangs out of her eyes. "I guess you're right."

"Just at least give me a little more time before you take off," I said.

"I don't have much time," Heather said.

"I don't need much."

Charlotte chuckled. "At the rate you're going I'm not sure I would get her hopes up."

I glared at Charlotte again.

"I'm just trying to push you to work harder. It will do you good," Charlotte said.

I reached out and hugged Heather. She embraced me back, but her body was so tense it was like hugging a concrete slab.

Heather wiped away another tear. "Okay, I'll wait."

"I'd keep an eye on her. I'm not sure you can trust her not to leave. The last thing we need right now is for the police to be hunting a fugitive." Charlotte eyed Heather up and down.

Peggy pointed. "And tell her no more tears. When other people cry, I cry, and I don't want to do that."

"Yes, for heaven's sake, no more waterworks," Charlotte said.

"Come back to the shop with me and hang out for a bit. It'll do you good to talk." I took Heather by the arm and guided her toward my place.

I made it halfway back to the shop when my cell phone rang. It was the number for Glorious Grits. The fact that I knew the number meant I had placed too many to-go orders.

"Why is Dixie calling me?" I touched my phone's screen.

Dixie didn't even let me finish saying hello until she said, "Where are you? You're supposed to be at the bake sale. I've just come from the church to retrieve more baked goods from the diner. Half the people who said they were coming haven't shown up and that includes you."

"Oh no, I forgot. I'll be there in two shakes of a lamb's tail," I said.

"You better or else I won't give you any more of that cherry pie that you love."

Chapter 23

Charlotte's Tips for a Fabulous Afterlife

Learn when not to spy on the living.
There are some things you just don't want to see.
Once you've seen them you can't un-see them.

"I don't like the look on your face. What's wrong?" Charlotte asked.

"I completely forgot about the bake sale. I told Dixie I would bring something." I adjusted the strap on my vintage Chanel flap purse.

Charlotte laughed. I knew why she was laughing. She thought I was a terrible baker. She was wrong though. I wasn't half bad.

"Well, no need to panic. It's not a big deal," Charlotte said. "Just go whip up something that you call baking. What time do you have to be there? And don't say five minutes."

"No, I have an hour." I looked at the time on my phone.

Heather was still standing next to me in a bit of a daze. Suddenly, she snapped out of it and looked at me. "You have to be there in an hour? What are you waiting on? Let's go bake something."

We rushed into the Buick and hurried toward my house.

"I have a good chocolate chip cookie recipe," I said.

Charlotte groaned. "Chocolate chip cookies? How boring."

"Well, it's all that I can come up with on such short notice," I said.

"Short notice? Didn't she tell you about the bake sale weeks ago?" Charlotte asked.

"You know what I mean," I said.

Charlotte sighed. "I suppose it'll have to do."

I steered the Buick onto my driveway, practically on two wheels. This was a baking emergency. We jumped out of the car and ran into the house. I had to hurry and get to the sale so that I could get back to the shop. I had a murder mystery to solve.

The four of us burst into my kitchen, making a mad dash for the cabinets. Heather and I grabbed the ingredients from the shelves and refrigerator. I pulled out a large mixing bowl. Heather and I dumped in the ingredients.

"Oh, this truly is a sight to behold," Charlotte said.

Peggy chuckled.

"Too bad I don't have any extra special items

to add to make this recipe something special."
I added the eggs.

"Perhaps you could give it a special name,"
Heather said. "That might make people think
it's fancy."

"How about Cookie's Fancy Chocolate Chip
Cookies?" I asked.

"That actually might work." Heather scooped
the dough onto the sheet.

"It'll have to do," I said, shoving the cookie
sheet into the oven.

In total we had forty-seven cookies after I ate
one of them. After all, my name wasn't Cookie
for nothing. Heather had flour on her cheek.

"I'm just glad that Dylan and Ken can't see
this," Charlotte said.

I placed my hands on my hips. "What is that
supposed to mean?"

She held her hands up. "Nothing, nothing
at all."

I grabbed the plastic storage container for
the cookies. Slipping on my Elvis Presley oven
mitt, I pulled out the cookies. Heather and I
stared at the cookies, willing them to cool off.
Once we couldn't wait any longer, I slid the
cookies off the sheet and into the container.
With the container of cookies in my hands, we
ran back out to the car.

"We have five minutes to get there," Heather
said, looking at her watch.

Heather and I slid onto the front seat of the

car. Peggy and Charlotte were already waiting in the backseat.

"I hate sitting back here," Charlotte said in her loudest voice possible.

"Deal with it." I cranked the engine.

"You'll never get there in time," Charlotte said.

"Thanks for the vote of confidence," I said.

She just said that because I'd been snippy with her. She'd started it.

As I pulled out onto the road, the tires squealed just a bit. If Dylan heard that he would definitely pull me over and probably give me a ticket. I tried not to speed . . . well, maybe five miles over the limit.

"I can't believe you forgot this in the first place," Charlotte said.

"Well, I have been a little bit busy," I said, steering the car around a curve.

"Yeah, you've been busy with me," Heather said.

Heather's sad face made my stomach twist into a knot.

"Look what you did now," Charlotte said. "You made Heather feel bad."

"Oh, I didn't mean anything by that, Heather."

She nodded but didn't answer. Now I felt terrible.

"Look what you've done now," Charlotte said.

"Yeah, it was all her fault," Peggy said.

I stared at them through the rearview mirror. They shrugged in unison. Partners in crime.

After the quick drive back into town, I pulled into the church parking lot and found a spot. I turned off the car and grabbed the plastic container. We rushed to the church and burst through the door, as if we'd been chased. Everyone in the space stopped and stared at us. I knew my face must have turned red at the attention.

Dixie ran over to us. "Oh, thank goodness you're here." She grabbed the plastic container and peered down. "I was embarrassed and worried that I wouldn't have enough stuff to sell."

"Well, I made my fancy chocolate chip cookies," I said.

She lifted an eyebrow. "Fancy cookies?"

"Yes, of course," I said with a sheepish smile.

"What makes them fancy?" she asked.

"The way I put the ingredients into the bowl," I said.

Dixie shook her head. "Well, it's just important that you got them here."

She headed over to the table and put down my cookies for purchase. I thought it seemed to be a good turnout. The table was full of baked goods, cakes, cupcakes, and all kinds of desserts.

"Now can we get out of here? We have other things we need to do," Charlotte said.

Yes, we had other things, like getting back to

the shop, but I couldn't leave without making a purchase.

"I just need to pick up a dessert and we can leave," I said to Heather.

She followed me as we made our way over to the table to find something with the least amount of calories. Yeah right, that would be impossible. I should just pick out the best looking thing and forget about the calories. After all, this was for charity. I picked up pretty decorated cupcakes with pink frosting and white sprinkles on the top. There were only six of them, so it would keep me from eating a ton. I'd give the rest to Dylan. After picking up the container of cupcakes, I paid for the purchase and surreptitiously motioned for the ghosts to follow me. Charlotte and Peggy had been talking while I looked at the desserts. That was just as well. I hadn't needed Charlotte's wisecracks about the calorie content. Heather had been waiting by the door. She wasn't in the mood for eating sweets. I bought something out of obligation for Dixie and the charity.

On my way toward the door Mrs. Bachman stopped me. "Cookie Chanel, oh, it's lovely to see you. You bought my cupcakes. I hope you love them."

"I'm sure I will," I said with a smile.

"You must take a bite right now," she said.

Heather and I exchanged a look. "Right now?"

Mrs. Bachman stared at me from behind her thick eyeglasses.

"Okay, I guess."

Anything so I could hurry up and get out of there. I pulled the top of the container back and took out a cupcake. Sprinkles tumbled from the top and frosting was on my fingers. I peeled back a bit of the paper liner and moved the cupcake toward my mouth to take a big bite. In one swift movement Charlotte swatted at the cupcake. Her energy had been powerful enough that it actually knocked the baked good out of my hand. The cupcake landed on the floor with a splat. I couldn't believe that Charlotte had knocked it out of my hand.

"What in the world did you do that for?" I asked. "Have you lost your mind?"

When I realized that I had spoken to Charlotte out loud, I looked at Mrs. Bachman. Her small mouth hung open as she stared at me. She looked at me as if I had lost *my* mind.

"I didn't knock that out of your hand," Mrs. Bachman said. "You must have dropped it. Though I admit the whole thing was really strange. It looked as if someone knocked it out of your hand."

Charlotte had really gotten me into trouble this time. I was completely flustered and didn't know what to say.

"Cookie, I saw someone messing around with those cupcakes. I just can't let you eat them."

Yet she could let me buy them? What was she thinking? Oh, now I got it. If I bought them no one else would eat them. Had someone really messed with the cupcakes? I would have to wait until I got outside to ask questions. Right now I couldn't talk in front of Mrs. Bachman. I picked up the cupcake and put it back in the container, closing the lid.

"I'm sorry. I just can't eat them right now. We're in a hurry, you understand, right, Mrs. Bachman?"

She continued to stare without an answer.

When I hurried out the door, I said, "What is going on, Charlotte?"

"I saw a woman do something to the cupcakes."

"Why didn't you say something right away?"

"There she is right now." Charlotte pointed. "I saw that woman do something. It looks like Marie, doesn't it?"

"How would you know with the big ugly black hat she's wearing and the dark sunglasses?" I asked.

"Apparently people have things for hats around here," Peggy said.

"Are we even sure it's a woman. Remember?"

"I'm not sure of anything anymore," Charlotte said.

Regardless if this was a man or woman we had to follow this person.

I rushed over toward my car. "What makes

you think that she was doing something to the cupcakes?"

"She sprinkled something on top of them. I think it was meant to look as if it was part of the sprinkles, but really it's probably poison."

"That's a huge assumption," I said.

Charlotte and Peggy got into the backseat. Heather and I jumped into the front seat. I cranked the engine of the Buick and headed in the direction where we'd seen the car pull out. Now that I was on the street, though, I couldn't spot the little blue car anywhere.

"I think she got away," I said.

"Now what will you do?" Heather asked.

"I don't know. I suppose I'll just have to go back to the shop."

"You definitely will want to give Dylan those cupcakes so that he can have them tested for poison."

"If there's nothing wrong with the cupcakes he will really think I'm out of my mind," I said.

"I think that's a small price to pay for answers," Charlotte said.

I turned right and headed toward the shop. I was more confused now than ever.

"How do we know she didn't put something on the other items? What if she tried to kill everyone there?"

"Oh, it was just you she wanted to get rid of," Charlotte said.

"How do you know?" I asked.

"I was watching this woman and spotted her when she walked in. She waited until she saw which item you were buying, then made her move. She entered the building right after you did, so I think she'd been following you. Right after she did the deed, she left," Charlotte said with a click of her tongue.

"You're supposed to tell me this stuff right away, Charlotte," I said.

How did she expect me to solve a crime when she didn't keep me informed? I supposed I would tell Dylan about the cupcakes, but it wasn't going to be easy explaining the whole bake sale debacle. Things just kept getting crazier and crazier. After a few seconds, we pulled up in front of my shop again.

"What type of poison could she possibly have put on these cupcakes?" I asked.

"Well, since I'm not an expert on poison," Charlotte said with a bit of snarkiness in her voice, "I really don't know."

Heather stared straight ahead as if she were in another world. Was she even aware that I was speaking?

Peggy leaned forward from the backseat. "Oh, I know. What if it was rat poison or something like that."

"Oh, that's a good one," Charlotte said. "I bet that's what it was."

The thought of ingesting rat poison didn't sound pleasant. What a horrible way to die, and to think this woman was trying to do that to me. I was dealing with an extremely demented person.

"This is an extremely dangerous and serious situation," Charlotte said.

She didn't have to tell me. I was well aware of how dangerous this was. Unfortunately, I didn't know what else to do about it. How could I make this stop? Not investigating the murder wasn't an option.

Chapter 24

Cookie's Savvy Tips for Vintage Clothing Shopping

If the price is right don't be afraid to buy a garment with a small stain. You might be able to get it out, but be aware it could have been there for years, making it impossible to remove.

Once inside my shop, Heather plopped down on the settee. She released a big sigh and leaned her head back. Brianna had just left.

"Hey, that's my seat," Charlotte said.

I waved my hands to stop Charlotte. Charlotte scowled and took a seat on one of the armed chairs by the dressing room. She folded her arms across her chest. Charlotte looked like a pouting three-year-old.

"These chairs aren't nearly as comfortable," Charlotte said, shifting from side to side.

As if it really mattered. She was a ghost. It wasn't like her bottom would fall asleep. Besides, I thought those chairs were plenty comfortable. Sure, I'd picked them out because they were cute, but comfort had crossed my mind too.

I placed the potentially poisoned cupcakes under the counter until Dylan could pick them up or until I had a chance to take them to him. I didn't want anyone possibly eating them. Wind Song jumped down from her window seat and strolled over to Heather. She jumped onto the settee and placed her paw on Heather's arm.

"That is so sweet," Peggy said.

"Grandma Pearl obviously wants you to feel better," I said.

Grandma Pearl meowed and we laughed. Heather rubbed the cat's head. Next Grandma Pearl hopped down from the settee, scrolled over to the counter, and leapt up.

"Oh, she has a message for us." Charlotte hurried over.

I pulled out the Ouija board. "What do you want to say, Grandma Pearl?"

"That I'm going to prison for life?" Heather asked.

"Of course not." I grimaced. "Right, Grandma Pearl?"

She placed her little paw on the planchette and moved it around the board. The plastic pointer glided silently across the top. We watched intently to make out the words. After a few more seconds she stopped and looked up at me.

"*Look for the knife?*" I frowned. "Grandma Pearl, they already have the knife. I saw pictures of it."

She picked up the pace this time, moving the planchette around the board faster than ever.

"Looks like she is frustrated with you." Charlotte pointed.

"*Where it came from?*" I asked.

"She wants you to look for where the knife came from? What does that mean?" Peggy asked.

"I think she means where the knife was purchased," Charlotte answered.

"I guess I haven't looked for where it came from. Where does someone buy a knife like that?" I asked.

"At a sporting goods store?" Heather suggested.

Heather hadn't seemed interested in what Grandma Pearl had to say until now. This was a good sign. Maybe she was feeling a bit more hopeful.

"Looks like we need to go window shopping," I said.

"What are we waiting for?" Charlotte motioned toward the front door.

I looked at the time on my phone. "I guess I could close a little early."

"You've spent too much time trying to help me," Heather said. "It's pointless."

"Nonsense." I placed the board back under the counter. "I don't even want to hear you talk that way anymore."

"Me either." Charlotte narrowed her eyes at Heather.

"I'll third that statement," Peggy said.

I closed the shop in a hurry and we headed outside.

Heather stopped on the sidewalk. "I just remembered something I need to do at the shop."

"Are you sure you're not just saying that? You won't take off, will you?"

She held her hand up. "I promise."

"I don't know if I trust her." Charlotte narrowed her eyes and looked Heather up and down.

I couldn't watch her all the time. She was a grown woman and didn't need a babysitter.

I sighed. "Okay, but I'll call you soon and let you know what I found."

Heather forced a smile. "I'll hold you to that."

We watched as Heather turned and walked to her shop. She waved as she stepped inside.

"Do you believe her?" Peggy asked.

"Yes, I do. Heather wouldn't lie to me," I said.

Charlotte's right eyebrow lifted. "I guess we can trust her. You should keep tabs on her more."

I gave a little salute. "Absolutely."

The sporting goods store would be closing soon. We hurried into the Buick. Too bad it wasn't close enough to walk. Since the store was closing in twenty minutes, I didn't want to take a chance on not making it. Luckily, I cruised through every green light and got there in record time. It was as if fate had stepped in and served me up a favor. I parked the car in the lot and hurried toward the door.

"Fifteen minutes left to look around. That should be plenty of time," I said, looking at the time on my phone.

When I walked into the store the female employee at the register looked at me. Her face drooped when she saw me. Faint music played in the background. It looked as if I was the only customer in the place.

"I suppose she was hoping no more customers would come in this evening," Charlotte said.

"It's not like I'm buying anything," I whispered.

"That makes it even worse." Charlotte laughed.

Another male employee was pretending to straighten things on a shelf. It looked as if he was just counting down the minutes until time to lock the door. He cast a frown my way.

"Excuse me, can you tell me where I can find the knives?"

He stared and pointed. "At the back of the store."

"Thanks." I hurried toward the back.

"I'm surprised he didn't tell you to hurry up," Peggy said.

"That would be rude. I don't think he's that keen on being fired," Charlotte said.

Soon I spotted the glass display case. What were the odds I would find the exact style knife?

"Don't you think the police haven't checked to see where that knife came from?" Charlotte asked. "I bet Dylan would be highly offended if he knew you were here second-guessing his work."

"That's why we'll never tell him," I said out of the corner of my mouth so no one would see me talking.

Peggy laughed.

I scanned the knives in the case, but nothing looked like the one I'd seen in the photo. There were small ones, large ones, and every size in between.

"Don't be discouraged, Cookie. You gave it a try," Charlotte said.

Peggy shrugged. "It was a long shot."

I couldn't help but feel discouraged. Heather was ready to leave town, and a killer was still on the loose. Someone else could be killed at any time. Someone like me. Movement caught my attention. An older gray-haired man appeared from a back room. At least he didn't look angry when he saw me.

He stepped over to the counter. "May I help you find something?"

I sighed. "It doesn't look as if you have the knife I was looking for."

He studied my face. "What kind of knife were you looking for?"

"It has a special design on the handle." I gestured with my index finger.

As if he would be able to figure out the design by my gesturing.

"We have a catalog that might have it." He motioned over his shoulder.

"They have a catalog of knives?" Charlotte asked.

"I'd love to see the catalog," I said.

"You'd better make it snappy." Charlotte looked at her watch. "You only have twelve minutes before the store closes. The employees up front will come back here and drag you out by your pretty vintage shirt."

The man stepped into the back room, leaving me alone to talk with the ghosts.

"Plenty of time," I said.

"I have a good feeling about this," Peggy said with enthusiasm.

A few seconds later the man returned with a large book. He plopped it on top of the glass display case. "Here you are, young lady."

"My heavens, who knew there were so many weapons. That's a little scary," Charlotte said.

"I hope there's more than knives in there," Peggy said.

"Thank you." I flipped the cover open.

"This will take forever." Charlotte leaned against the display case.

I knew my time was limited and I'd have to flip through hurriedly. However, there was no way I would give up that easily. I'd just have to turn the pages quickly.

"Maybe if you can describe the knife I can help you," the man said.

He probably didn't want me to look through the whole catalog. I didn't want to, either, but I needed to know.

"Well, it has a gold scroll pattern on the handle." I didn't stop turning the pages.

"I think I might know the knife. There's a manufacturer who makes the design specifically." He turned the catalog around and flipped halfway toward the back. He stopped on the page and turned the catalog around so that I could see the photos. "Is it one of these?"

"Oh, you'll never figure this out," Charlotte said. "Look at all of them."

Yes, they were all similar. "Do you sell many of these?"

I decided to change my plan.

"Yes, we have them here. Don't have any in stock right now. They sell well so as soon as one comes in it's out the door," he said.

"Do you remember selling one recently?" I asked.

"It doesn't matter if he sold one recently. The killer could have had it for years," Charlotte said.

Charlotte could be such a downer sometimes. If a person bought one recently, and that person happened to match the description of one of my suspects, it was likely that I would find the killer.

"How recent?" the man asked.

"I suppose what I really want to know is if a certain person purchased the knife." I studied his face.

"That doesn't work either." Peggy leaned closer. "You'll have to describe every suspect."

I didn't have that many suspects so it wouldn't take that long. Though I knew the clock was ticking.

"I don't know if I can help you with that." He shifted from one foot to the other.

"I think he's getting anxious," Charlotte said.

I figured I'd take a chance and ask if a woman had purchased the knife. He looked around as if someone might hear. No one was nearby. At least no one that I saw. One of the employees could be lurking nearby for all I knew. A woman's voice came over the loud speaker.

"The store will be closing in five minutes. Please bring your purchases to the front."

"That means they want you to get out," Charlotte said with a click of her tongue.

Yes, I was aware. I had to hurry.

"Please, it would help me a lot," I said.

"What did she look like?" He scanned the surroundings.

"He knows something." Charlotte pointed. "I can tell by the look in his eyes."

The man did have a strange look now.

"She had blond hair that comes down below her shoulders. Wide set green eyes and she wears a lot of jewelry," I said. "I think she's probably five foot seven inches tall and I guess around one hundred forty pounds. Maybe in her mid-fifties."

"You have been around Dylan too long," Charlotte said.

"After that description I could pick her out of a lineup," Peggy said.

The man stared at me. "Yes, someone matching that description bought the knife about a month ago."

"Do you know the woman?" I asked.

"The person paid with cash," he said.

"That isn't exactly a direct answer," Charlotte said.

"What about surveillance footage?" I crossed my fingers that he'd give the answer I wanted.

"The police are working on getting that, I think." He closed the catalog.

"You should know that Dylan is working on that," Charlotte said.

Dylan hadn't mentioned that to me. Though I suppose there were things he couldn't share about the case. Something that important, though, I figured he'd give me a hint. The other male employee was lurking around the corner, watching me.

"Thank you for the information," I said.

"You're welcome," the man said.

"I wish he could give you more information," Peggy said as she rushed along beside me.

I hurried toward the front of the store. The woman at the register glared at me. The male employee had moved and was waiting at the door, ready to lock it. He twirled the keys in his hand. As I reached the door, the woman walked from behind the counter and joined the man at the front door.

"Remind me to never go there that close to closing time," I said under my breath. I rushed out the door.

The employees didn't stop there. They followed me out, as if making sure I wouldn't try to enter again.

"Are they still standing there?" I asked.

Charlotte looked back. "They're going back in now."

"Thank goodness," I said.

"Something doesn't seem right." I unlocked the car and climbed behind the wheel.

"What do you mean?" Charlotte asked from the passenger seat beside me.

"It's just a feeling, I guess." I turned the ignition and pulled out of the parking lot. "I think I need to call Dylan and ask about the knife."

"You're probably just upset by the way the employees rushed you," Peggy said.

"I hope that's all," I said.

After a short distance driving, I pulled over to the side of the road and dialed Dylan's number.

"I was just getting ready to call you," he said when he answered.

"Is everything okay?" I asked.

"Just fine. I wanted to hear your voice."

"Aw, that's so sweet," Charlotte said.

"What a dreamboat," Peggy said.

Dylan was on speakerphone. Charlotte hated not being able to hear all of a conversation. Now I hated to tell him that I had called to ask about the case. Not that I didn't want to talk with him about other things too. It was just that I had been so consumed with the case lately that I seemed to forget about everything else. I needed to remember the people around me needed my attention.

"How about dinner tonight?" he asked.

"Only if I'm making," I said.

"Don't scare the man away," Charlotte said.

I glared at her.

"Oh, and tell him about the cupcakes."

Dylan chuckled. "That sounds perfect, but . . ."

"Oh, there's always a but," Charlotte said.

"Maybe he doesn't like your cooking?" Peggy said.

"I thought we could check out the new restaurant," Dylan said.

I was just glad that it wasn't my cooking that made him pause. At least I hoped he wasn't suggesting a restaurant because of my cooking skills. I'd tell him about the cupcakes once we got to the restaurant.

"I'd like that," I said. "I'll meet you there."

"I'll be there at seven, if that's okay?"

"Sounds great," I said.

"Was there something else on your mind?" he asked.

"I can talk to you about it tonight."

"If you're sure," he said.

Better to do it in person.

"I'm sure."

Chapter 25

Charlotte's Tips for a Fabulous Afterlife

Location, location, location. Mansions.
Why do you think mansions are always the most
haunted? Granted if you pick an abandoned one,
that will turn against you.
Seriously pick a nice location to haunt.

I hurried home to change for my date. My dress of choice was a beautiful Christian Dior black cocktail dress from the early 1950s. Black beading covered the bodice and the bust had a flame cut. The upper chest and neckline along with the sleeves had sheer black fabric. Perhaps I was a bit overdressed for Sugar Creek, but I didn't care. If I didn't dress up now I'd never get the chance because I rarely went anywhere fancy enough for most of the clothing I loved. The dress's material had a faint floral print in a darker shade of black. I managed to get the back zipper up. This dress reminded me of something I'd seen Lucy wear in several episodes of *I Love Lucy.*

My shoes were black strappy heels and my purse was white with a black floral pattern. It gave just the right amount of pop to my outfit. After spritzing some of my new Chanel perfume on my wrists and neck, I headed outside and slipped behind the wheel. With one twist of the key I cranked the engine. As usual Charlotte and Peggy were with me. Charlotte riding shotgun and Peggy in the backseat. They had on their finest outfits, as if someone would see them.

"I can't go to a nice restaurant and not be dressed up," Charlotte said.

Peggy wore the red dress that was her favorite. Charlotte had taught her how to change an outfit with just a single thought. Charlotte switched her outfits so often she was like a chameleon. Dylan said he was running a little late. I wondered if it had anything to do with the Morris case. If it did, I would for sure try to get that information from Dylan. I'd just made it to downtown when my cell rang.

"That might be Dylan." I whipped the car into the Dairy Queen parking lot and pulled my phone from my purse.

I didn't recognize the number. Normally, I would let the call go to voice mail, but something told me I should answer.

"This is Cookie Chanel," I said, trying to sound professional.

"I think you need to go to the lake," the female voice said.

"Excuse me?" I asked with a raised eyebrow.

"Who is it?" Charlotte asked.

"Who is this?" I asked.

"You need to go to the lake," the woman repeated.

"I don't know what you're talking about."

"It must be a wrong number," Peggy said.

"There's a cabin. Morris took his lovers there. The killer is there now."

My eyes widened.

"Where is this cabin?" I asked.

"It is by the lake. Beside the tallest oak tree."

"That doesn't help me much," I said. "Why don't you call the police?"

"No, don't call the police. The killer will be waiting for the police to show up and shoot at them."

"The killer has a gun?" My voice shot up.

The woman didn't respond.

Charlotte scoffed. "Well, killers usually have weapons, Cookie. It shouldn't come as a shock."

"Hello?" I asked.

There was no answer. The mystery female had ended the call.

"What was that all about?" Charlotte asked.

"The woman said she thinks the killer is at a cabin at the lake. Should I go there?"

"I don't know, Cookie, this could be a setup. You should call Dylan," Charlotte said.

"Yes, it could be, but what if it's not. She said don't call the police because the killer will try to kill the police. I can't put Dylan in that kind of danger."

"This is risky, Cookie. I don't think you know what you're getting into," Charlotte said.

"Now I'm even more nervous," Peggy said.

I pulled back onto the road and headed toward the lake. "I'll just have to take my chances."

"This will not end well." Charlotte sighed.

At the light I turned right instead of left toward the restaurant. I'd have to call Dylan and tell him I'd be late. If he was late maybe he wouldn't even notice I wasn't there yet. He'd wonder why and I wouldn't be able to tell him the reason for my tardiness. My cell rang.

"Maybe it's Dylan," I said.

When I looked at the screen, Ken's name popped up. Of course I didn't have time to chat, but what if he'd found out something about the case.

"Hello." I knew my voice sounded frazzled.

"Cookie, I just thought I'd check in with you. How are you?"

"Oh, Ken, I don't have time to talk right now. I'll call you later, okay?" I pushed the gas just a little more.

"Sure. Are you sure everything is okay? You sound strange."

"Everything will be fine. Call you soon."

I ended the call, although I knew Ken would worry now. The last thing I needed was for him to want to come to the cabin with me. I wanted to keep everyone from danger.

"Poor Ken. Always getting the short end of the stick," Charlotte said.

"Don't make me feel worse than I already do," I said.

The landscape changed from buildings to dense trees. Soon I reached the entrance for the lake. I knew the area the woman had told me about, but not well. There was a cabin by an old oak tree that had been there for years. I wasn't sure anyone ever used the place. The road stopped at the dirt path, and I would have to walk the rest of the way to the cabin.

"I still don't think you should do this," Charlotte said.

"Yes, I agree. It's a bad idea," Peggy said.

I parked the car and cut the engine. "I realize this isn't a wise choice, but I can't send the police in there. What if Dylan was hurt or heaven forbid killed? I'd never forgive myself."

"You could ask someone else to go with you?"

"Who would I ask? I definitely don't want Heather involved in this. She's already in too much with this case. I will be careful; I promise." I opened the door and climbed out.

Charlotte and Peggy followed me as I headed down the dirt path. Pine trees surrounded me as I disappeared deeper and deeper into the vegetation. The sound of a snapping branch stopped me in my tracks.

"Oh my heaven. What was that?" Charlotte clutched her chest. "Is someone shooting at us?"

"There are probably a lot of wild animals around here," Peggy said.

I didn't need that reminder. I was already nervous enough. "No one is shooting at us, Charlotte. It was just a tree branch."

"They're not shooting at us yet," Charlotte said under her breath.

Up ahead was a clearing, and I knew the cabin was right past it. As I neared the area, I moved over to a larger tree, hoping it would offer some kind of cover. The last thing I needed was for the killer to know I was coming. I should have changed my clothing before going on a hiking adventure. There had been no time though. With the way things were recently I should keep sleuthing attire in my car for a quick change.

"Did you ever stop to think that the person who called could be the killer?" Charlotte asked.

"I suppose I hadn't thought of that until you mentioned it," I said.

"It's not too late to turn around," Peggy said.

I stood a little taller. "No, I will go through with this."

"Aw, that's my Cookie, always tough and strong." Charlotte smiled. "Foolish, but tough and strong. A little stubborn too."

I released a deep breath and stepped out from the protection of the oak tree. A million thoughts ran through my mind. I envisioned a large man stepping out onto the cabin's porch.

He would spot me right away and run out to grab me. I tried to shake off the daydream. The ghosts eased along beside me as I made my way to the cabin. Now I stood at the bottom of the porch steps.

"Now what?" Charlotte asked, peering up at the front door. "You can't just knock on the door."

"No, I suppose I can't do that." I stared at the cabin.

"Maybe no one is even here," Peggy said.

"True. I should go peek in the window," I said.

Charlotte gestured with a sweeping motion of her arm. "Well, what are you waiting for? Might as well get it over with."

I knew Charlotte well by now, and I sensed when she was nervous. This was one of those rare times. I placed my foot on the bottom tread. The wood creaked under the weight of my step. I cringed at the noise.

"You have to push forward. Hurry," Charlotte said. "The longer you wait the worse it will be."

With a grimace on my face I rushed up the stairs. With each placement of my foot the steps groaned. Thank goodness I was now at the top. Unfortunately, the wood floor made the same creaking noise as I walked across.

"You might as well ring a bell announcing your arrival," Charlotte said. "Can't you quiet your steps?"

I tiptoed across the floor toward the window, weaving around a clay pot with a dead plant in it.

"Someone clearly doesn't have a green thumb." Charlotte scowled as she looked at the brown drooping leaves.

I released a breath when I reached the window. This ordeal was far from over though. Now was not the time to relax.

Old lace curtains that had at one time probably been white but were now a pale yellow hung in front of the glass from the other side. At least I could see a bit through them and into the cabin. A kitchen table with a few chairs around it sat directly in front of me. Over to the left were an old plaid sofa and a brown leather recliner. No one was in sight. Apparently I'd made this trip for nothing.

"It looks like no one is here," I whispered.

"If no one is there, why are you whispering?" Charlotte asked.

The ghosts were right beside me.

"Someone is here," the female voice said from over my shoulder.

Peggy screamed before I even had a chance to turn around. The next thing I knew someone had grabbed me from behind.

Chapter 26

Don't be afraid to mix styles from different decades.
Just don't go overboard with fads.
Classic styles look good together no matter what year
the garment came from; some designs are timeless.

"I knew this was a bad idea," Charlotte said.

That wasn't what she'd said earlier. Charlotte had practically forced me to go.

When I got a look at the woman's face, I realized Patricia Chrisman had been the one who grabbed me.

"Get off of her," Charlotte yelled.

Too bad Patricia couldn't see the ghosts. Maybe that would scare her away.

"What do you think you're doing?" I asked.

"I should ask you the same question." Patricia yanked on my arm.

"We have to do something," Peggy said in a panic as she paced across the porch.

Patricia was surprisingly strong. Did she lift weights? Maybe I should consider something more than jogging or yoga. Somehow she managed to open the cabin door and shoved me inside.

"Get out of there, Cookie. Once she has you trapped in there you'll never get out." Charlotte raced in after me.

It was too late for that now. Patricia locked the door behind her. When I started to walk right around her to leave, she pulled out a large knife. I held my hands up and stepped back.

"You're not going anywhere," Patricia said.

"There's no need to do anything crazy." I moved a couple more steps backward.

Patricia glared at me. "Oh, I think there is."

"You've gotten yourself into quite a pickle, Cookie," Charlotte said.

"This is no time to talk about food," Peggy said.

Charlotte glared at Peggy.

"Oh, sorry," Peggy said. "I'm just so scared I can't think straight."

"You killed Morris, didn't you?" I asked.

Patricia had a strong grip on the knife. It was obvious Patricia had a thing for knives.

She stared at me for a long bit, and said, "I had no other choice."

"Why do you say that?" I pressed.

"A confession will get you nothing if you're dead, Cookie. Please be careful." Charlotte stood by Patricia, staring down at the knife.

I knew Charlotte was trying to think of a way to get the knife out of Patricia's hand.

Patricia inched my way. I backed up until I bumped into the wall. There was nowhere else for me to go. This looked like the end for me. Patricia was right in front of me now. Her eyes were locked on me. She moved the knife up to my face. The blade was ice cold against my skin.

"I would cut your pretty face, but unfortunately now I have to do much more than that." She moved the blade along my cheek.

The cold of the steel sent an equally cold chill down my spine. Charlotte and Peggy were both taking swings at Patricia. Their fists went straight through her. Patricia seemed to notice something was going on because she frowned and surveyed the surroundings.

"Why do you think you have to do something to me?" My voice quavered.

"I think that's kind of obvious, Cookie, don't you?" Charlotte said. "And don't you dare cry."

Well, yes, it was obvious, but I had to keep the conversation going so maybe she wouldn't kill me. Plus, just because my voice quavered didn't mean that I was going to cry.

"You like to think of yourself as a detective, huh?" Patricia asked. "Maybe you should stick to vintage fashion."

"It's a little late for that now," Charlotte said. "This woman is nuttier than a pecan pie."

"Ask her more about why she killed Morris," Peggy said.

"Why did you kill Morris?" I followed Peggy's instructions.

Patricia pointed the knife at my chest. My heart beat faster. It seemed almost hopeless that I would get away from her.

"He wanted to end things between us." Her eyes seemed blank, as if she spoke but really wasn't even there.

She was probably replaying the murder over in her mind. No doubt she'd enjoyed it.

"So he broke up with you?" I asked.

Charlotte moved closer to Patricia. "Honey, when it's over, it's over. There are other fish in the sea. No need to pine away over one man."

Patricia frowned again and looked to her right. It was almost as if she sensed Charlotte. Too bad Patricia couldn't see or hear Charlotte. Maybe I could get away.

"Yes, he said he couldn't see me, but I didn't believe him. He was just saying that because my husband had confronted him."

"That sounds like good enough reason." Charlotte rolled her eyes.

"Well . . . he was your husband," I said, trying not to make her angrier.

"I told him I would leave my husband. He said that didn't matter."

"Take a hint, honey," Charlotte said. "He just wasn't that into you."

"Look, you can put that all behind you now," I said.

"She can't do that. The woman is going to prison where she belongs." Charlotte pointed at Patricia.

Well, I knew that, but I didn't want to remind Patricia at a time like this. What was one more murder to her when she'd already killed one?

Patricia shook her head. "No, I can't do that. And I can't allow you to tell anyone."

"I promise I wouldn't tell anyone," I said.

"Oh yeah, right, like she's going to believe that. We have to think of something else." Charlotte paced across the floor.

A squeaking noise caught our attention. Patricia froze. I recognized the noise, but I hoped she didn't. Someone was on the porch. No one knew I was here. Maybe it was a raccoon.

"Is someone with you?" Patricia asked. "You'd better not lie to me."

So she did recognize the noise.

Charlotte and Peggy rushed over to the door and looked out.

"Heather is here," Charlotte said.

Oh no. Heather had to leave. Should I tell Charlotte to have Heather run? Would Heather finally be able to tune in to her psychic abilities? I didn't care if Patricia thought I was crazy. I didn't want her to know Heather was out there and go after her. She couldn't kill us both at the same time though, right? Before I had a chance to debate any longer, Charlotte and Peggy disappeared out the door. Patricia backed over to the door. She kept her eyes on me and the knife pointed in my direction.

"Don't make any funny moves," Patricia warned.

I had to do something to stop her from hurting Heather. What was going on out there? Patricia moved over to the window. Charlotte and Peggy reappeared inside.

"Heather looked in the window and saw what was going on so she took off," Charlotte said.

I mouthed, "Where did she go?"

Charlotte frowned. "What?"

Oh, for heaven's sake. I had hoped she'd be able to read my lips.

"What did she say?" Peggy asked Charlotte.

Charlotte shrugged. "When did sheet soap?"

"That doesn't make sense." Peggy's eyebrows pinched together in confusion.

I shook my head and repeated, "Where did she go?"

Charlotte frowned. "Where did sheep go?"

I glared at her. "Where did Heather go?"

"Around the side of the house," Peggy answered.

"Cookie, you really need to learn to enunciate." Charlotte shook her head.

Patricia was looking out the window, but she still had the knife pointed at me. I wasn't sure I was willing to risk trying to get it away from her. She'd already proven that she knew how to use the thing. Patricia turned her attention back toward me.

"You're up to something. I can sense it." She eyed me up and down.

"I don't know what you're talking about," I said, trying to act innocent.

Another noise caught my attention. I had no idea where it came from, but I suspected it was from the back of the cabin. Patricia didn't seem to notice this time. It could have been an animal for all I knew. I was holding out hope that it was Heather. Maybe she was trying to get in the house. Though I didn't want her to get hurt, I still needed help getting away from this mad woman. Patricia was still looking out the window, trying to see if someone was out there. The knife was pointed at me so there was no chance I could get away from her.

"Did you hear that?" Charlotte asked.

I nodded.

"We'll go check it out." Charlotte motioned for Peggy to follow her.

They disappeared down the small hallway. Now I was alone with Patricia. That thought sent a shiver down my spine.

Patricia turned her attention back to me now. "I suppose it was an animal."

"Yes, there are a lot out here," I said.

Another noise caught her attention. She studied me. "Are you doing that?"

"I haven't moved," I said.

Patricia stared out the window again. While she was distracted, I scanned the room, hoping to locate some kind of weapon to help me fight her off. Unfortunately, there was really nothing that was readily available to me. The cabin was sparsely decorated. Across the way was a lamp on the table in the living area. Possibly I could use that to hit her, but what if it didn't work? That would only make her angrier. No, it was too risky to take that chance.

As I peered around the room, I noticed a bottle of what looked like white powder sitting on the table in the dining area. Immediately, I thought of the cupcakes. She was definitely the one who had added something to them. And this was the poison sitting right there in plain sight. Seeing that bottle sent a shiver down my spine. Knowing how evil she was, and that she could murder someone with such ease, made me sick. It looked as if I was going to be her next victim after all. If she couldn't poison me she would just stab me. The same fate as Morris.

Once I was gone there would be no one to figure out the murder for Heather. She would be in jail for life. Sure, Dylan would be on the case, but Patricia would probably come after him too. That made my stomach churn more. Looking to my right, I spotted a big floppy hat thrown haphazardly on the sofa. There was a pair of large black sunglasses on the table next to the sofa. They were the same ones she had worn while putting the poison on the cupcakes at the bake sale. Yes, now I knew for sure that she had been the one responsible for that.

Patricia turned around. Her eyes settled on me immediately. I was sure she noticed that I was looking at the items. She smirked and I knew she was happy with her evil feat.

"You tried to poison me," I said. "Why would you do that?"

Of course I knew the answer. She was evil. I wanted to keep this conversation going as long as possible. Maybe it would give me a chance to think of a way out of this.

"I thought it would be an interesting way for you to go. Less for me to do." A slow wicked smile spread across Patricia's face.

"You could have killed someone else with the cupcakes," I said.

She smirked. "That was a chance I was willing to take."

That I believed. Patricia had zero empathy for anyone. She was only worried about herself. She didn't care who she had to kill to get what she wanted.

"You won't get away with this. The police will figure it out. They'll know you killed me too."

She laughed. The sound was like an icy hand running up my back. "They haven't figured it out yet, so I don't expect they ever will."

She was way more confident than she should

be about Dylan's ability to solve this crime. That made fury bubble inside me. I had to stop her.

Where were the ghosts? What was going on back there? What would I do if it was Heather? If Heather was back there she would come out of that hallway. That was a big if though. Patricia would see her if she came down that hallway. I had to get Patricia to look in the other direction. Of course that would mean I would have to move. Patricia wasn't letting me go anywhere. Charlotte and Peggy returned down the hallway.

"Heather is in that room. She came through the window." I'd rarely heard Charlotte so panicked.

"What will we do?" Peggy asked.

Charlotte peeked down the hallway. "Oh no. She just opened the door. Patricia will see her."

"This is terrible." Peggy touched her forehead with the back of her hand.

It was as if Charlotte read my mind when she said, "I know. I'll cause a distraction."

She ran over to the table by the sofa. There sat a small brass lamp. Charlotte rushed over to the lamp. Cold air whirled around the room, and I felt my energy drain. I knew Charlotte was using the energy around her to be able to move that lamp. Charlotte stretched her arm out and toward the lamp. With a loud crash the lamp hit the ground and rolled a short distance. Charlotte smiled with pride.

Patricia jumped, and without thinking about

turning her back on me she raced over to the lamp. This was Heather's chance and I hoped she took it. Out of the corner of my eye I spotted Heather. Her eyes were wide and she placed her index finger up to her mouth to indicate for me to remain silent. No problem there. I was forgetting to even breathe. Heather had a vintage pullover sweater in her hand. I recognized it from my car. It was with other pieces of clothing I'd placed in the back to take to the shop. What was she doing with it?

"What is she doing?" Charlotte asked with a raised voice.

Peggy covered her eyes with her hands. "I can't look."

Heather was right behind Patricia. Though Patricia had the knife in her hand, she had stopped pointing it at me. She had no clue that Heather was right behind her. The ghosts and I watched in stunned silence. Peggy had uncovered her eyes. I knew she couldn't keep from looking. Heather lifted the sweater high over Patricia's head and yanked it down. I ran over and tackled Patricia. She screamed as she hit the floor. Now I had her pinned to the floor, but I had no idea what would happen next.

"You have to find a way to tie her up," Charlotte said.

"Heather, do you see any rope?" I asked as Patricia struggled to get free.

"Don't forget to get that knife in case she gets free." Peggy pointed.

"There has to be something we can use," Heather said, looking around the cabin.

"Maybe you should just call the police. I'll sit on her until they get here," I said.

"No offense, Cookie, but I don't think you're strong enough to keep her down," Heather said.

Heather was right. I was already growing tired. The adrenaline had allowed me to tackle her down in the first place. Fear was creeping back in now, and I might lose control of her soon.

"We will both have to sit on her. The police are already on their way." Heather rushed over and lay across Patricia's legs.

Patricia groaned and used a few colorful phrases to impart her displeasure.

"Wait until the police get a load of this scene." Charlotte laughed.

I imagined we looked ridiculous, but this was life or death.

Patricia struggled with the sweater over her head. "I can't breathe."

"So, I'm glad you found me," I said as we sat on Patricia.

"I knew something was wrong. You accidentally dialed my number and left a voice mail. I heard you talking to the ghosts," Heather said.

"Why do I keep doing that?" I asked.

"Why do you keep doing a lot of things?" Charlotte asked.

Patricia wiggled underneath us. I was getting tired. How long until the police arrived?

"Get this sweater off me," Patricia yelled.

"Look out," Peggy screamed.

Patricia had almost reached the knife. Heather had forgotten to pick it up. Heather reached for the knife and managed to get a hold before Patricia could get it in her hand. If she'd been able to take a swipe at one of us, she probably would have gotten the upper hand again. That was a close one. Sirens echoed in the distance. As the seconds passed they came closer and closer.

"Police, open up," the officer yelled.

"We can't open the door; we're sitting on top of the perp," Heather yelled.

A few seconds later and the door burst open. Officers stormed in with guns drawn. Dylan was the first one in. His shirt was covered in mud and he had a slight limp. The officers weren't the only ones there. Ken was with Dylan. What was he doing here? Our eyes met. For a brief time he stared in shock. Next Dylan raced over to me. Another officer placed Patricia in cuffs. Ken watched from a distance. Heather and I were able to stand now. The cops pulled Patricia up from the floor.

"Impressive work," Dylan said with a smile. "Why does she have a sweater over her head?"

"I thought we did a good job," I said. "I couldn't have done it without Heather. She saved me by putting the sweater over Patricia's head. After that I tackled Patricia."

Heather blushed. "It was you who figured out Patricia was the killer. Without you I would be going to prison soon."

Dylan embraced me in a hug. "You shouldn't have come out here alone."

Yes, I figured I would get dirt all over my dress from Dylan's dirty shirt. I hugged him tighter. Life was meant to get a little dirty sometimes.

"What happened to you? Why are you limping? Are you okay? I'm guessing it has something to do with your dirty shirt," I said.

"I took a little tumble on my way here. I'll be fine." He brushed the hair away from my face.

"All's well that ends well," Charlotte said.

"That was real fatal attraction," Heather said, brushing off her pants.

Catching a killer was dirty work, but someone had to do it. I stepped away from Dylan. Looking down at my clothing I realized I'd managed to keep my fabulous dress clean. Even better. Maybe this day would turn out okay after all.

"I have another question," I said.

"What's that?" Dylan asked.

"Why is Ken with you?" I asked.

Everyone looked at Ken.

"Thank goodness you asked. This was driving me crazy," Charlotte said.

"I'll let Ken explain," Dylan said.

Ken moved closer to us. "After talking to you I decided to come looking for you. Whatever you were into didn't sound safe. I happened to spot your car and Dylan's. I took a chance and walked into the woods. That was when I spotted Dylan. He'd tripped and couldn't get his foot out from under a log. I just helped him up."

Dylan wrapped his arms around Ken's shoulders. "He did more than that. He saved me and you and Heather."

"Handsome, smart, and now a hero," Charlotte said.

"Thank you doesn't seem like enough." I hugged Ken.

His cheeks turned pink. "I'm just glad everyone is okay."

"Let's get you all out of here." Dylan guided me toward the door by placing his hand on the small of my back.

We walked outside with Dylan. Heather hugged me again as we watched the police put Patricia in the back of the police cruiser. Patricia made rude gestures our way. Ken and Dylan were talking. This was one of the few times I'd ever seen them exchange words. Usually, they stared at each other and nodded.

"That woman is pure evil," Charlotte said.

"I'm so glad my life can be back to normal now," Heather said.

"Why would you want it back to what you call 'normal'?" Charlotte asked.

I was glad Heather didn't hear that remark.

Dylan pulled me to the side. "Can I talk with you privately for a minute?"

I looked at the ghosts. Charlotte quirked an eyebrow but stayed put.

"Is something wrong?" I asked.

The ghosts were still eyeing us suspiciously.

"Are they still here?" Dylan peered around.

I knew he meant the ghosts.

Gesturing with a tilt of my head, I said, "They're right over there. Why do you ask?"

"I have information about Peggy's murder." His voice was low as if he still didn't trust that the ghosts weren't next to us.

"You do?" I asked with wide eyes. "What did you find out? Is Peggy not supposed to know?"

The ghosts had figured out that we were discussing them. Dylan and I shouldn't have looked at them so many times. Now they were standing right next to us.

Charlotte tapped her foot against the ground. "Exactly what is going on over here? You keep looking at us for a reason? Cookie, you're not very subtle."

"Dylan has information about Peggy's murder," I whispered. "They're here now. Sorry."

Dylan looked to my right. "Yes, that's right."

I thought it was adorable that he was trying to talk with the ghosts.

"Well, let us have it." Charlotte waved her hand. "What did you find out?"

"I'm scared." Peggy's eyes were full of fear.

"No need to be worried," Charlotte said. "You're already dead. What's the worst that can happen now?"

Charlotte certainly had a way with words.

Dylan turned his attention to me again. "We've located her killer. He confessed to his niece before he died. She'd been covering for him all this time. I've ordered a search for her remains."

"Wow, after all these years. What will happen to him? Who was it?" I asked.

"Yes, I want to know why he did it," Charlotte said.

Peggy stood a little straighter. "Yes, I want to know. I can handle it."

I knew this news was a lot for her to take.

"Her boyfriend, Steve Walker, killed her at the theater. He dumped her in the woods. He said Peggy was cheating on him with another man. I suppose he snapped." Dylan frowned.

"Yes, you could say that," Charlotte said. "What is with everyone and the jealousy?"

"That's terrible," I said, glancing at Peggy.

"That wasn't true," Peggy said. "I wanted to break up with him because he was so controlling. I remember it all now."

Charlotte attempted to pat Peggy on the shoulder. "Honey, we can talk about this. It'll be okay."

"So his niece was covering for him. Will she face any charges for that?" I said.

"Well, I guess we'll see what happens. It's up to the DA," Dylan said.

"I don't like the sound of that," Charlotte said.

"Did you find out any information on Mike Harvey? Why was he creeping around?" I asked.

"I spoke with him. He was suspicious of Patricia, and wanted to alert me to her behavior. The guy was scared that she may come after him." Dylan ran his hand through his hair.

"She probably would have if she'd known he talked to you," I said. "By the way, on the table in the cabin there's a bottle of poison."

Dylan furrowed his brow. "And how do you know this?"

"Well, because Patricia tried to poison the cupcakes I bought from the bake sale. She wanted to kill me long before I came to this cabin. The cupcakes are in my car." I was glad I had decided to put the cupcakes in my car earlier, thinking I would give them to Dylan after dinner.

"Also, the disguise she wore is in the cabin. Sunglasses and a big hat."

"Thank goodness Patricia wasn't clever enough. She couldn't pull one over on us," Charlotte said with a wink.

I owed Charlotte big time for what she'd done by spotting Patricia sprinkling the poison on the cupcakes. If not for her I would have been a goner. She would remind me of that plenty of times too.

"I'll be right back," Dylan said as he waved to another officer.

"I suppose my time here is now over." Peggy looked down at her black and white saddle shoes.

"It doesn't have to be. Look at me. I'm staying around." Charlotte smiled.

"That's because Cookie needs you," Peggy said.

"Why does everyone keep saying that?" I asked. "I'm fine on my own. I can take care of myself."

Charlotte raised an eyebrow. "As if I need to explain why you need help."

"There's no use trying to talk me out of it," Peggy said.

I kept my eye out for a bright light. In the past other ghosts had disappeared that way. Nothing out of the ordinary appeared. Just the blue sky with the sun setting over the horizon.

Without saying a word Peggy walked away. Charlotte and I exchanged a look.

"What is she doing?" Charlotte asked.

I shrugged. "I have no idea."

"Let's find out." Charlotte took off, motioning for me to follow.

Charlotte and I soon caught up to Peggy.

"What are you doing?" I asked.

"I've decided to go back to the theater. I like it there. After all these years it feels like my home." Peggy continued walking.

"You know you don't have to do that, right?" Charlotte asked.

I looked back at Dylan and Ken. Dylan shrugged his shoulders and held his arms up. Clearly he wanted to know what I was doing. I pointed beside me. Dylan nodded. Thank goodness he understood about the ghosts and believed me. Would he tell Ken about my weird talent?

"I don't see any other option. We can't stay with Cookie. She has her own life and doesn't need us hanging around all the time."

Charlotte frowned. I saw the realization in her eyes. Was she now thinking the same thing? I wasn't going to let Charlotte think that I didn't want her around.

"Charlotte goes back and forth between the worlds. That's her choice to come back and see me. We're friends. Friends visit each other." I smiled at Charlotte.

"Yes, that's what friends do." Charlotte winked.

"Really? Do you think I could do that too? Could I stop back in the theater any time I want?" Peggy asked.

I looked to Charlotte for the answer to that question.

"Of course you can. Any time you want." Charlotte draped her arm around Peggy's shoulders. "Come on. I'll show you the way."

"Thank you for everything, Cookie," Peggy said.

"This isn't good-bye, right?" I asked.

Peggy smiled. "Yes, I'll be back soon."

Charlotte waved as Peggy and she walked away. Soon they'd disappeared into the woods. I wasn't sure if Peggy would really return, but I hoped that she would come back to visit. Ken and Dylan were still talking when I walked back over.

"This seems like an intense conversation," I said.

"Just discussing last night's game," Dylan said.

I smiled. "Good. I'm glad."

I'd given Dylan the cupcakes and he took them as evidence against Patricia. The police had also retrieved the poison from inside the house. The charges against her would be plentiful. With any luck she'd never get out of prison.

The police pulled away from the cabin. Relief fell over me as I watched them drive away with Patricia. I hoped Heather was right and that things could now be back to normal. As normal as life could be while living with ghosts. Ken had been there to help Dylan. I hoped they could put their differences aside now and become friends. It looked as if they were off to a good start. Would Sugar Creek once again be a charming Southern town? Probably until the next murder.

COOKIE CHANEL'S STRATEGY
for VINTAGE SHOPPING ON A BUDGET

You don't have to spend a fortune to buy vintage items. Plus, you can even score designer pieces without breaking the bank. So put away those credit cards and follow these easy tips to a frugal, yet fun vintage shopping experience.

1. Buy vintage items that were once trendy. People may think the style has come and gone, but you can always bring something back in style. An item can be paired with something classic and make a fun, playful look. By purchasing something less in demand you can save money. Though never try to bring those polyester suits back. Those are off limits.
2. Look for coupons or ask for a discount. Some stores might offer a group coupon online or feature a percentage off in an advertisement. Check your local paper for special offers. Also

stores might have certain days of the week when they give a certain percentage off purchases. Be on the lookout for bargains.

3. Shop for off-season items. If you're willing to wait to wear something until the season rolls around again, then you could definitely find some bargains. A lot of stores will mark down items as the season comes to an end. You can snag a cute sweater for next winter in the middle of July.

4. Shop online at auction sites or other vendors selling vintage items. Not only do they offer rare items and a large inventory, but they also offer bargains. You can find just about anything you're looking for online. Though remember you can't try on and a lot of places have a no return policy. So check the measurements.

5. Accessories are budget friendly. If you can't swing the price tags for a full wardrobe, consider buying smaller items like belts, purses, scarves, or jewelry. These items can add color and style to any outfit and they won't break the bank. Adding a colorful vintage handbag can change any ensemble from drab to fab.

6. Don't forget sometimes you can buy vintage clothing in unexpected places. Consider looking at flea markets, yard sales, antique shops, and other unexpected stores. Since they don't deal mainly with vintage clothing, these places might be more willing to negotiate on prices. You just might find a hidden gem.

7. Though most vintage shops or thrift stores won't offer coupons, it doesn't hurt to ask if the price is negotiable. Some shops will offer discounts after a certain number of days. So if you can wait you might get lucky and return for the item when it will be marked down.

8. Be on the lookout for vintage clothing swap meet-ups. There are other vintage clothing owners out there who are interested in trading. Maybe you have a garment that isn't right for you but might be perfect for someone else. You might get lucky and find the perfect piece you've been looking for.

Grandma Pearl's Advice *for* Cats

Attention cats: avoid séances. You never know when a ghost might take over your body. The ghost will find ways to use you to communicate with the living humans. Then, if a ghost gets the upper hand you might be in a power struggle for which cat food tastes best.

Have some variety in your diet. Do you have to eat fish all the time? Ghosts get sick of that. Especially little old Southern ladies who are set in their ways.

Do you really need to groom your fur so often? The hair balls are horrendous. Now I know being neat and tidy is of the upmost importance, but this action seems excessive.

Furthermore, chasing mice and other rodents? This is vile, darling. Southern ladies don't act this way. You should show grace and tact. At the very least wait until the thing follows nature's course and then retrieve it, but this batting it around with your paws for hours just for amusement is sadistic behavior.

The one good thing I can say is, while still

atrocious, at least you have a litter box. It could be worse; you could have to do your business on the front lawn for the whole world to see. Poor Rover down the street has no privacy. I suppose that's payback, though, for the time he chased us up a tree.

Until next time, dear, remember always watch out for the rocking chairs. You do not want your tail caught under one of those.

ACKNOWLEDGMENTS

Many thanks to my family and friends. They embrace my quirkiness. Love you all! Also thank you to my editor, Michaela Hamilton, and my agent, Jill Marsal.

Don't miss the next irresistible
HAUNTED VINTAGE mystery by Rose Pressey

FASHIONS FADE, HAUNTED IS ETERNAL

Coming soon from Kensington Publishing Corp!

Keep reading to enjoy an excerpt . . .

Chapter 1

Gnarled and twisted branches draped down over the cemetery's gates, as if they wanted to reach out and grab every person who walked through. The location for the photo shoot gave me the creeps. I wasn't sure why the photographer, Tyler Fields, had insisted on taking the photos in the spooky Sugar Creek Cemetery.

He'd called me just a week ago and said, "Cookie Chanel, I need you to style the models. We don't have time to waste, so I expect you to be ready on short notice."

Normally, I would have told him there was no way I could work with such little warning. This was a big opportunity for me, though, so I'd agreed. After all, owning my own vintage clothing store It's Vintage Y'all in Sugar Creek, Georgia, had made me somewhat of a vintage clothing expert. So that was how I'd found myself standing in the middle of the cemetery on a beautiful fall day.

Tyler had posed the models beside the black iron fence. Headstones and mausoleums filled the background of his photos. He stomped over to the beautiful women and showed them exactly how he wanted them to stand. The longer he waited for the models to get the poses just right, the redder his face became.

Tyler was much shorter than the models, standing on his tiptoes to reach their hair. He had sandy-brown hair that parted to the side and fell over his eyes. He didn't seem bothered by this obstruction of his view. Perhaps that was why the models' poses seemed skewed. The white short-sleeved polo shirt and olive green cargo pants he wore hung loosely on his thin frame.

I suppose since this was for the Halloween issue of *Fashion and Style Magazine,* a spooky graveyard was the perfect setting. Though that didn't make it any less scary. Seeing models photographed wearing the vintage outfits that I had picked out was a big highlight of my life. I'd never thought I'd be asked to style the models for the October issue.

Some people might find it ironic that a cemetery gave me the cold chills, considering I had a ghost attached to me and she was currently critiquing the photographer's skills.

"That pose is all wrong . . . but he didn't ask me," Charlotte said with a click of her tongue.

Charlotte Meadows was a ghost and one of

my best friends. Not to mention fashionable and a former socialite. Today she wore a silk abstract-printed belted dress by Emilio Pucci. The colors were coral, turquoise, and black, which flattered her brunette hair. The dress was short-sleeved and reached just above her knees. It was a good thing she was a ghost wearing her black Christian Louboutin heels, because there was no way she would have been able to walk through the grass in those things as a living being.

Charlotte had been attached to some of her vintage clothing that I'd purchased at her estate sale. She'd been by my side ever since. Lately, it seemed as if I'd had a revolving paranormal door of ghosts in my life. Nevertheless, I was hoping my current location didn't attract a new spirit.

Tombstones and mausoleums surrounded us with etched prayers on plaques and statues of angels guarding over the dearly departed. Spanish moss hung from the tree branches like curtains. The smell of damp earth drifted across the gentle breeze. At least it was the middle of the day and not dark out. There were several models, assistants, and the photographer around, so my ghost friend wasn't my only companion. I'd styled the models in sweaters, wool skirts, and walking shorts with knee socks for a perfect fall look. My favorite outfit was the head-to-toe Ralph Lauren. The plaid wool high-waist walking shorts, blue-and-green-striped sweater, and knee-high socks were all of pieces from the 1980s, but looked modern and current. Some styles were timeless.

I kept the 1980s style going by wearing a dark blue Calvin Klein shirtdress. The gold buttons down the front and the string belt with gold tassels meant accessories weren't needed with this outfit. My blue sandals were by Guess and had a canvas vamp with corkscrew sole. Charlotte said I could be one of the models, but with my height at just five-foot-two, I knew she was just being nice. Compliments from Charlotte didn't come often so I'd take it.

We'd taken a short break, but the photographer had told the models not to get too comfortable. He had a tendency to be a bit harsh, although I'd heard he was good at his job. From the looks of the photos I'd seen in the magazine, I'd say that was accurate.

"If he barked orders at me I'd be out of here." Charlotte gestured over her shoulder.

"Unfortunately, I think the women will put up with it just to keep their jobs," I said.

I'd only been around Tyler for a short time now, and I already wasn't fond of him. Thank goodness he wasn't yelling orders at me. Charlotte stared in the direction where Tyler stood. He was doing something to his camera lens. If I knew Charlotte, and I thought I knew her well, then she was plotting something against Tyler. She enjoyed playing pranks on people when she felt they were misbehaving. She liked to do things like knocking stuff out of their hands, touching them, or turning off lights. The usual ghostly shenanigans.

"Charlotte, don't get any ideas," I warned with a point of my finger.

She held her hands up. "What? I wasn't planning anything . . . I certainly wasn't scheming to knock the camera out of his hands. Oh, maybe I should push over that tripod."

"He's already frustrated enough. Don't push him."

Charlotte mumbled something that I couldn't understand. That was probably for the best. Movement to my right caught my attention. A man had just walked out from behind one of the tall headstones. What had he been doing back there? Where had he come from? There was only one entrance to the graveyard and that was at the front. Based on the tall headstones around him, I guessed his height at six feet. He had wide shoulders and a muscular physique. His blond hair was cut so short that he almost appeared bald. He wore black jeans, a black leather jacket, and black boots.

"Who is that?" Charlotte asked.

"That's what I'd like to know," I said. "He just came out from behind that tall headstone."

"There's something suspicious about that," Charlotte said. "We need to keep an eye on him."

I would definitely do that. The man was

headed toward the group of models who were talking while taking a break.

"Do you think he has bad intentions?" I asked. "I don't like the way he is walking toward them."

"This could be dangerous," Charlotte said.

"Maybe you should alert someone," the woman beside me said.

"Yes, maybe I should." My eyes widened when I realized a stranger was standing beside us.

How had she slipped up on us? Who was she? I hated to be rude, but I wanted to know who she was.

"Who are you?" Charlotte asked with a scowl on her face.

Charlotte, on the other hand, didn't hate to be rude.

"Pardon me, my name is Minnie Lynn." Dimples appeared on her round cheeks when she smiled.

"That's nice, Minnie, but that still doesn't tell us who you are." Charlotte eyed Minnie up and down.

I scanned Minnie's appearance at that point too. Minnie didn't have to answer completely for me to know that she was a ghost. Well, I suppose I didn't know for sure, but the fact that we were standing in a graveyard and Minnie was dressed head-to-toe in vintage clothing gave me a good clue. Minnie wore a long cream-colored dress from what looked like the 1920s. A cute cloche-style hat rested on top of her head. Brown hair peeked out from underneath.

Before she got a chance to answer, yelling caught our attention. The man who had appeared from behind the headstone was now arguing with Tyler. I wasn't quite sure what they were arguing about.

"Maybe we should move closer so that we can hear better," Charlotte said.

"What if they start fighting? We should probably stay clear of that," I said.

One of the models managed to get the man away from Tyler. The model and the man walked out of the cemetery.

The photographer walked back over to the area where he'd been taking photos before the break. "All right, everyone. Let's get back to work."

His words were so harsh and he barked the orders. I had nothing else to do other than collect the clothing that I'd allowed them to borrow once the shoot was over. Now I was anxious to get out of there. I watched as the assistant raced over and adjusted the clothing on the models. Tyler glanced back at me and frowned. I attempted a smile, but he turned his attention back to the models. Perhaps he didn't want me here. Tyler started snapping photos and calling out orders to the models. The model who had walked the man out from the cemetery came rushing back over. Tyler glared at her.

"I'm ready," she said, taking her place next to the other women.

Tyler didn't speak to her directly. He just started snapping photos again.

"I wonder what that is all about?" Minnie Lynn said, capturing my attention once again.

Charlotte whipped her focus on Minnie. She walked over to Minnie, standing right in front of her. "Now I didn't see you enter the cemetery, so who are you? Are you with the magazine?"

Minnie looked at me, as if to say please get this woman to leave me alone. I was sorry, but I couldn't help her. Once Charlotte got on something she wouldn't let it go.

"Well, we are curious who you are. It's not often that we meet strangers in the middle of the cemetery," I said.

"Often? Try never." Charlotte eyed Minnie up and down.

Minnie looked down at her cream-colored pumps. There were no stains on her shoes. No signs that she'd been walking through the soft earth of the cemetery; of course there wouldn't be any if she truly was a ghost.

"I don't know why I'm here." Her voice was soft and low.

Charlotte quirked an eyebrow. "I don't believe that."

My gaze traveled from Minnie's feet to the top of her head. I took in every detail of her vintage clothing. After all, that was my job.

When my eyes fell on the long strand of pearls around her neck I knew she was here because of me. I'd recently picked up pearls at an estate sale identical to the ones she was wearing now.

"I suspect I know what's going on with Minnie."

Her big brown eyes widened. "You do?"

"Do you know that you're a ghost?" I asked.

She stared at me. "Yes, I know."

"Well, why didn't you say so? I'm a ghost too." Charlotte gestured toward herself.

Now it was Minnie's turn to eye Charlotte up and down. "I can tell."

Charlotte scowled. "What's that supposed to mean?"

"Don't be defensive. I saw absolutely no one other than Cookie look at you. That means they can't even see you."

Charlotte's expression eased. "Oh, I guess that's a good reason."

"Wait. How did you know my name?" I asked.

"I've been hanging around since you bought my necklace. I just didn't show myself until now."

I raised an eyebrow. "You have?"

"Why show up now?" Charlotte placed her hands on her hips.

Movement caught our attention, stopping the conversation. The models were walking away from the shoot and headed toward the cemetery's gates.

"What's happening, Krissy?" I asked, hoping that was her name.

Yes, now I remembered her full name—Krissy Dustin. She'd told me earlier when I'd given her the outfit. She was the model who had walked the muscular guy out.

"Tyler said he needed a break from us. I guess we weren't doing what he wanted." She pushed her blond hair away from her face.

"Where did he go?" I asked.

She pointed. "I guess he's taking a walk."

When I looked out across the cemetery, I spotted Tyler walking in the distance. He disappeared around one of the tall oak trees. Krissy joined the other models outside the cemetery.

"He'll get over it," Charlotte said with a wave of her hand. "Now back to the conversation with Minnie."

Once again, the conversation was interrupted when a gunshot rang out.

Charlotte gasped and clutched her chest. "Heavens to Betsy. What was that?"